PRAISE FOR ROBERT J.

D0942569

FIRST EDITION

Distributed in Canada by
Publishers Group Canada
76 Stafford Street, Unit 300
Toronto, Ontario, M6J 2S1
Toll Free: 800-747-8147
e-mail: info@pgcbooks.ca

Distributed in the U.S. by
Consortium Book Sales & Distribution
34 Thirteenth Avenue, NE, Suite 101
Minneapolis, MN 55413
Phone: (612) 746-2600
e-mail: sales.orders@cbsd.com

Library and Archives Canada Cataloguing in Publication

Wiersema, Robert J., author

Seven crow stories / Robert J. Wiersema.

Short stories.

Issued in print and electronic formats.

ISBN 978-1-77148-395-7 (paperback).--ISBN 978-1-77148-396-4 (PDF)

I. Title.

PS8645.I33S49 2016   C813'.6   C2016-905897-2

C2016-905898-0

Shelfie

A **free** eBook edition is available
with the purchase of this print book.

CLEARLY PRINT YOUR NAME ABOVE IN UPPER CASE
Instructions to claim your free eBook edition:
1. Download the Shelfie app for Android or iOS
2. Write your name in **UPPER CASE** above
3. Use the Shelfie app to submit a photo
4. Download your eBook to any device

CHIZINE PUBLICATIONS
Peterborough, Canada
www.chizinepub.com
info@chizinepub.com

Edited by Samantha Beiko
Proofread by Leigh Teetzel

Canada Council   Conseil des arts
for the Arts   du Canada

We acknowledge the support of the Canada Council for the Arts which last year invested $20.1 million in writing and publishing throughout Canada.

ONTARIO ARTS COUNCIL
CONSEIL DES ARTS DE L'ONTARIO
an Ontario government agency
un organisme du gouvernement de l'Ontario

Published with the generous assistance of the Ontario Arts Council.

Printed in Canada

SEVEN CROW STORIES

ChiZine Publications

ROBERT J. WIERSEMA

SEVEN

CROW

STORIES

For the lost, and the gone . . .

GRATEFUL

It was just getting dark when I saw her, a little past nine o'clock.

I had just come around the bend when my headlights fell across her; it was almost too late.

I was driving south along that stretch of the Malahat just past the summit, where the highway shrinks to one lane in either direction, a sheer rock wall on one side of the road and a drop several hundred metres down to the cold waters of Finlayson Arm on the other. There was no shoulder: she was standing in the lane itself, pressed against the base of the rock wall. I jerked my wheel to the left, and a Nanaimo-bound trucker in the other lane swerved and laid on his horn. Checking for headlights in my rearview mirror, I slammed on the brakes, sliding to a stop just past her.

I broke out in a clammy sweat, and I could barely hear over my heart as she opened the passenger door.

"Are you nuts?" I stormed at her before she could speak. "You could have gotten yourself killed. You could have gotten *me* killed."

"I'm sorry," she flinched. She was leaning on the seat and bending into the car, and it looked for a moment like she might recoil, disappear into the night. All I could see of her in the half-light was a dark nimbus of hair and the ungainly protrusion of her backpack.

"What were you doing out there?" I was gradually calming down, but it hadn't reached my voice yet. She still seemed wary, unmoving and tense, wound tight as a watch-spring.

"Well, my friends, they went on ahead, and . . ." She paused.

It was the quaver in her voice. All of a sudden I was on her side. "They just left you here?"

There was a movement that I took to be nodding. "I don't think they really meant to, though. They were, you know, drinking a little. . . ."

"Some friends," I muttered, catching a sudden flash of headlights in my mirror at the same moment we were almost blasted onto the rocks by a souped-up truck.

And again, a horn.

"Okay," I said, keeping my eye on the mirror. "Where are you headed?"

"All the way to Victoria," she said, as if it were some sort of hopeless quest.

"Hop in," I said, clearing my stuff off the passenger seat. "Let's get out of here while we still can."

She folded herself into the compact seat with an agility that some people attribute to teenagers; I don't remember ever being that flexible. She stuffed her knapsack in around by her feet, and as soon as her door was closed we were doing eighty, both of us still in one piece.

"Thanks a lot," she said, turning to face me. "You can just drop me off wherever. I'll figure it out from there."

I shook my head. "No, that's all right. I'm headed right into town. I'll get you where you're going."

"I'm grateful. It's a relief not to have to worry about it." She brushed her hair back from around her face.

In the ambient light from the dashboard and the sky, I could see that she was a pretty girl—dark hair, dark eyes, dark features, a little turn at the ends of her mouth that made her seem to be smiling. From my reading I would say that she had a dark Irish look to her, but I've never been to Ireland, and my entire impression of her was based on sidelong, half-lit glances, so I have no idea how accurate that would be.

"My name's Murray," I said, a little awkwardly. "I'm sorry I gave you such a hard time back there."

"No, I know how stupid it was to just be standing there. . . ." She shook her head. "I'm Jenny."

"Good to meet you, Jenny. Is there any sort of music you like?" I asked as I reached to eject the Grateful Dead CD.

"No, this is fine," she said, before I could press the button.

"We could listen to the radio."

"No, this is cool. Just continue as you were before you were so rudely interrupted." I glanced over at her and saw her smiling at me.

Not pretty. Beautiful.

Brett Mydland started singing "I Will Take You Home" in the pause that followed.

"Appropriate," she said.

"So tell me about these friends of yours," I said. "What were they thinking, just ditching you on the Malahat?"

"It was just a few of us. We were headed up to Cowichan for the night. Bit of a party—sort of a graduation thing, you know? Stacey's folks have a place up there on the lake." I nodded. I remembered very well the blur of parties that surrounded my high school graduation.

"Where are you graduating from?"

"Oak Bay."

I nodded again. "I graduated from Reynolds."

"Really? When?" She seemed oddly excited by the fact that we had high school graduation in common.

"Seven years ago."

"So what have you been doing since then?"

"The only thing I could do when I finished school: more school."

She nodded knowingly. "Anyways, we were headed up to the lake and, I don't know, I guess I got separated. I just want to get home."

"Well, I'll get you there."

There was obviously something that she wasn't telling me, but there was no way I was going to try to force it from her. I assumed that her friends had ditched her, and right away I was back in high school, going to parties where I wasn't invited, where I was ignored, desperate to find somewhere, anywhere, to fit in.

She smiled.

"So are you going to school in the fall?"

"Yeah. That's the plan, at least." She shrugged, as if the whole thing were out of her hands. "What about you?"

"Me?"

"Yeah. Are you done school, or . . ."

"Yes, indeed. Seven years and two degrees and all of a sudden I'm Mr. Fitzgerald, high school English teacher." I plumped myself up in the seat, mocking an effort to look important.

"That's cool." She sounded genuinely enthusiastic.

I shook my head.

"What?"

"I guess I'm sort of like you, out there tonight." I gestured at the darkness around the car. "I have *no* idea how I got here."

"You don't want to be a teacher?"

"It'll pay the bills, at least. Assuming I ever get a job. And if I can pay the bills then I can finally move out of my parents' basement. . . ." I wasn't really sure what I was going to say until I had already said it.

"Well, what did you want to do?"

I shrugged as if I didn't know.

"What did you go to school for, then?"

I took a deep breath. "I started out with an English degree because I figured it'd help me be a better writer. And when that didn't happen, I figured I'd go for an education degree, put it to some use. At least then I'd be able to eat."

"You wanted to be a writer?"

I nodded.

"So what happened?"

I faked a wry chuckle. "That's the funny part. I have absolutely no idea. It's like I woke up one morning and that whole part of me, all my drive, all my dreams, it was just gone. And I was—" I put on a booming baritone this time "—Mr. Fitzgerald, high school English teacher."

She didn't laugh. "Were you any good?" she asked.

"You get right to the point, don't you?"

She shrugged.

"I honestly have no idea anymore. I thought I was. Well, at first I used my writing to . . . I don't have the happiest memories of high school. I used writing these stories as my way of getting even." Glancing toward her, I saw a rueful half-smile of understanding settle on her face. "And when I first got to university I started writing these poems. Some of them even got published. I used to think I was good. That I had 'potential' with a capital P. I don't know, though."

"What happened? Why did you stop?" She pulled her legs up to her chest, sort of folded herself together.

"I didn't do it on purpose. It just sort of drifted away. I got a job so I wouldn't have to get a student loan, I started thinking about grad school, all sorts of things, until it just didn't seem very important anymore. The worst thing is, I didn't even notice it happening, and then one day it was just gone, and I wasn't that person anymore. I'd become someone else. Someone I didn't know."

"That's sad." She nodded like she understood. "It's kinda like those stories you see in the paper, you know the ones: seventeen-year-old honours student, bright future ahead, scholarships out the wazoo, dies in fiery car wreck days before graduation. Lost potential. That sort of thing."

I nodded slowly. "Sort of. Maybe that's the better way to go, though. You don't just fade away. You don't have to watch yourself just fade away." I glanced over at her. "Is there something you really want to do? Something that you *need* to do, with a passion?"

"I want to be a doctor," she said, without hesitation. "I've known ever since I was a little kid that I wanted to help people. That's why I'm going to university."

"Yeah. That's the way that I used to feel about writing. Then I got to here." I glanced at her again. She was staring at me, thoughtful. "You want a piece of advice? Don't let this happen to you. Take what you want and really go for it. Don't let it die, like I did."

She shook her head. "Not a chance."

It was that smile that brought me plummeting back to earth. "Well." I forced a chuckle. "That was your valedictory address. . . . Maybe I should be a guidance counsellor."

"Don't sell yourself short."

"What?"

"I think you've got a lot of passion. You can hear it when you're talking about the passion you think you don't have. I think you've just misplaced what you're looking for. It hasn't died. You just need to find it again."

I don't know why, but I shut her out. I knew the truth of what she was saying, the wisdom—it was something that I had told myself countless times. I just couldn't make myself believe it. "Yeah, maybe," I said. "Listen, where am I going?"

There was a moment of silence. "Uplands," she said, in a quiet voice.

We passed the rest of the drive without a word.

(

"The next left," she said tersely, just after we passed through the gates into Uplands. And then, after I turned: "And right." I turned again, and she said, "It's the place at the end of the block."

I pulled up in front.

It was a huge stone house, probably a hundred years old, with a roundabout driveway behind a set of high gates. "Home sweet home," I muttered, trying to break the tension.

"Don't hate me because I'm beautiful," she snapped back, reaching between her feet and pulling her knapsack into her lap.

"Hey," I said, turning to her. "I'm sorry that I cut you off back there. It wasn't very polite of me."

She shook her head. "No, it's really none of my business. You just seemed so unhappy."

"No, not unhappy." I tried, but I couldn't think of another adjective and I gave up. "I'll get over it."

"I hope so," she said. She opened up the door and stepped out. Leaning back in, she said, "Thanks again for the ride. I really appreciate it." Turning away, then turning back as if in afterthought, she said, "Good luck."

"You too." I smiled at her. "And congratulations."

"Thanks."

As she was about to close the door I call out to her. "Hey."

She leaned back into the car and I stretched in my seat toward her. "Listen, do you want to go, I don't know, maybe get a cup of coffee or something?"

She smiled broadly, but shook her head. "Thanks, but . . . I need to get home."

I nodded, not having expected anything else.

Not disappointed. Not really.

Closing the door, she hefted her knapsack onto her shoulder and walked through the gate. I watched as she walked up the driveway, the darkness of her slipping into and between the pools of shadow, only starting the car as she disappeared up the front steps.

I drove around for a while before I went home, hoping that my parents would both be asleep by the time I got there.

⸗

I was late coming up from the basement for breakfast the next morning. Mom and Dad were both sitting at the table, empty bowls from cereal already on the floor being fought over by the cats, half-empty cups of coffee at their elbows. They had split up the morning paper and were pretty engrossed, but they both looked up as I came in.

"You got in late," Dad said.

I nodded, pouring myself a coffee.

"Did you have any luck?"

"Well, Duncan's not hiring for sure. They've had to lay off fifteen teachers in the district, so there wasn't much point, but I did leave a resume. Cowichan just opened up their on-call list, but there are about seventy people ahead of me on it. Maybe Nanaimo, though. They're building some schools up there, so . . ." I crossed my fingers. "They won't know until September anyway."

Mom pulled a new section of the paper across the table. Dad asked, "Any plans for this afternoon?"

I shook my head. "Same old, same old. Retool my resume, maybe go for a swim."

"Oh, no," my mother muttered into the newspaper, shaking her head. "People are so bloody stupid. Listen to this: *'Fiery Crash Kills Four. A group of four Oak Bay High School graduating students died near the Malahat summit at 7 pm yesterday, according to an RCMP spokesman, when the car they were driving lost control and left the road, plunging to the rocks above Finlayson Arm. Alcohol is suspected to be a factor. . . .'"*

I couldn't breathe. I couldn't speak. The whole world seemed to stop, and I felt myself grow cold.

Jenny . . .

The day before what would have been graduation for the four students, there was a memorial service in the auditorium at the school. I couldn't get in, and I watched the ceremony, along with several hundred other people, on the big-screen televisions they had brought out and set up on the front lawn. The colours were bleached out from the sun, and the sound wavered, but it was more than I could take.

I think I was the only person alone at the service. Everyone else was clustered into small knots of grief—girls in sunglasses holding one another as they cried black streaks down their faces; boys who had no knowledge of loss awkwardly circling one another or uneasily cradling one of the crying girls, unsure of what to do with their hands, unsure of what to do with their mourning.

In the heat of my car, sweat beading on my face, I wept.

I drove down to Dallas Road, pulled into a parking slot and turned off the engine. The water was a blinding sheet of light in the afternoon sun.

I sat there for the longest time. I tried to understand, but nothing made sense. I wanted to think that I had imagined the whole thing, that I had dreamed the whole trip home, but it was easier to believe what I knew to be true than to try to deny it, to accept the reality of that night, the dark ride, taking her home.

It didn't make any sense, but I knew it was the truth.

Later that night, I drove past her house, parking a little way down the block. The gates were open, and the driveway was full of cars, the house brightly lit. In the yard were the same constellations of mourning I had seen at the school. I almost went to the house, into that field of loss, up to the door itself, but stopped myself. What would I have to say?

How do you mourn someone you never knew?

I had never felt so alone.

The next day, the day of the funerals, the newspaper printed their graduation photos, along with their yearbook entries and remembrances of their classmates and friends.

Jennifer Carmichael. Honours student. Valedictorian. Planning for a career in medicine. Full scholarship to McGill . . . What was the phrase she had used? *Scholarships out the wazoo.*

To be honest, the photograph of her wasn't very good. It showed a very formal young woman, almost stern, in a dark gown with her mortar cocked back on her tied-back hair. I tore the article and photograph out and laid them on my desk.

That night, just before dark, I went to the cemetery. I brought flowers, and carried them by my side along the winding paths.

It wasn't hard to find her grave. There was a pile of flowers, an easel with a photograph of her. In this one, she was laughing.

The earth on the grave was slightly rounded, the turf still rough. There was no headstone, only a small marker.

Carmichael, Jennifer.

I stood beside her grave, trying to make everything make sense. It didn't work.

I set the flowers down gently with the others.

"Thank you again for the ride," she said from behind me as I stood up.

Of course I hadn't heard her coming, but I wasn't surprised to hear her voice.

"It was nothing," I said, as I turned toward her.

In the half-light of the dusk she was radiant, burning with an inner light so bright I could barely look at her.

"No," she said. "It was something. It was everything. You got me home."

I nodded. I couldn't do anything else.

"I was hoping I would see you again. I wanted to do something to thank you."

"I've got so many questions," I started.

"And I don't have any answers." She smiled, and the brightness burned my eyes.

I had to turn away.

"Here," she whispered, and I was aware of her near me, her presence. I felt her lifting my hand, opening my fingers, without any sense of her touch. There was no physicality whatsoever, just her burning presence. And a cold weight in my hand. "I want you to have this."

I lifted it up to look at it in the half-light. It was a silver pen, cool and smooth.

"But what . . ."

"Not everybody would have stopped that night. If it wasn't for you, I wouldn't have made it home."

I wanted to argue with her, but I couldn't.

"It's a fountain pen. It was a graduation gift from my grandmother. Maybe you'll be able to use it."

"But I . . ."

As I spoke, I could feel her presence all around me, a warmth that chilled me, and, for only the briefest of moments, the touch of her lips against my cheek, and her whisper in my ear. "Use it."

And then she was gone, and I was utterly alone.

✦

I was up before my parents the next morning. I skipped breakfast, and was on the highway before there was any other sound in the house.

I averted my eyes as I passed the Malahat summit, kept my gaze fixed on the taillights of the car in front of me until I was well past the pullout and the viewpoint, and the spot where the car had left the road.

I spent the morning retracing my steps from earlier in the week. I stopped at the Duncan and Cowichan school board offices and withdrew my resumes from their consideration. I requested my application at the Nanaimo District office be destroyed.

And then I started for home, the fountain pen on the passenger seat next to a new black notebook.

I was almost to the summit when I saw the scene of the accident. The fencing had been replaced, but no one had painted it yet and it stood out like a wound on the landscape. On the edge of the road, the too-narrow shoulder above Finlayson Arm, there were four white crosses, sunlight playing across them. Heaped around them were wreaths and flowers, gifts and ribbons.

There was no room to stop, and I don't know what I would have left if there had been.

How do you remember someone you never really knew?

I pulled in at the viewpoint at the summit. There were a couple of carloads of tourists taking pictures against the backdrop of the mountains and the water. It was a glorious day.

I put on the Grateful Dead CD I had been playing that night and I took off my seatbelt.

The sketchbook was new; I had bought it at Opus the day before, looking for something with lots of pages, lots of space.

I had taped the newspaper article, with her photograph, on the inside of the front cover.

I opened up the book, unscrewed the cap from the pen, and began to write.

It was just getting dark when I saw her, a little past nine o'clock. . . .

Seven for a secret,
Never to be told.

Tom Chesnutt's Midnight Blues

For Marla

What's the worst thing you can imagine? The worst punishment someone could wish on you? To forever be cut off from those pretty young girls, the ones who look at you like you're a god? To wander the world looking for peace, but never knowing a moment's rest? To have your finest song never be heard?

"Can I get the houselights up?" Tom Chesnutt muttered into the microphone as he fumbled with his guitar strap. He cleared his throat and tried again. "Hank, can you bring up the lights?"

Cheers washed over him as Hank brought up the bar's main lights. The crowd was on their feet—they had been for most of the night.

It took a moment for his eyes to adjust, for the figures on the other side of the spotlights to start to come into focus.

"This is an old song," he said into the mic, almost as an aside, as he tightened the G string. He made it sound off the cuff, but it was the way he introduced the song every time he played it. A couple of people cheered; they'd seen the show before, or recognized the words from the record.

"It's nice to finish a night like this with an old song," he continued, looking down the guitar's neck. "A song everybody can sing along to." He ran his pick lightly over the strings, listening to the tuning in the monitor. It was fine, but he fumbled with the keys a little longer. For effect. Playing it out.

More of the crowd cheered—people were starting to figure out what was coming. The sound of the crowd had changed; it was darker now, lower than it had been when he first took the stage. Two hours of cheering and drinking and smoking had taken their toll.

"It's been a good night for me, Victoria." The crowd exploded with the mention of their city's name, same way they always did. "Hope y'all have had a good time too."

He shook the neck of his guitar decisively and straightened up in front of the mic.

"This song's called 'Jolene.'"

The crowd roared, and Frank started beating out the rhythm heavy, almost a Bo Diddley beat.

Tom let the guitar hang loose around his neck, curled his right hand around the microphone and leaned in, closing his eyes as he sang against the backbeat.

{

From www.thewebmusicguide.com:

Tom Chesnutt – singer, songwriter, guitar

Born in Santa Fe, NM, but based for most of his career in Spokane, WA, Chesnutt met with early success as a songwriter, penning tracks which included "Love and Smoke," "Brokedown in Your Eyes," "Right Child" and "Tell-All Eyes," which charted briefly for Stanza in 1987. His early albums, though critically well-received, sold poorly. After a brief hospitalization following the death of his fiancée Emily Grace in 1999, Chesnutt burst to national prominence with the album *Emily's Song*. Recorded in three days, the album is widely regarded as a dark masterpiece in the tradition of Bob Dylan's *Blood on the Tracks* and Neil Young's *Tonight's The Night*.

{

He'd got to the bar a couple hours early, same as he always did. The place was a crappy little club right on the water that had once hosted bands, before they discovered that there was more money in techno and drunk university students. Now, the only time they cleared the DJ and his equipment off the stage was for a Very Special Event—namely someone the owner or promoter really wanted to see for themselves.

Tom didn't mind that: Very Special Event. Had a nice ring to it.

He had wandered around while the guys loaded in and got set up, watching the pretty girls and the pretty buildings, the boats and the water. He had to stop to rest a couple of times; two nights without sleep and he was running on fumes. He got back to the club for a quick soundcheck, then he sent the boys off to find some food while he bellied up to the bar.

The bartender, a kid with a shaved head and a pierced lip, was still setting up, but he was kind enough, thank you very much, to provide a bottle of Maker's Mark and a glass. Tom's needs were simple.

"Water water everywhere," he muttered as the bartender turned away. "Only whiskey fit to drink."

He drank slowly but steadily, savouring the flavour and the burn of the whiskey, relying on it to cut through the last of the pills, bring him down a couple of notches to let him play.

When he poured the first glass, his hand was shaking so bad he thought he might actually spill. A couple of drinks later and his hand was perfectly still, the jangle gone from just behind his eyes.

"Better living through chemistry," he muttered.

The bartender glanced down at him and Tom shook his head. "Just talking to myself."

Emily smiled at him from the empty bar stool to his right. *"Is that what this is, you and I? You still think I'm some sort of projection?"*

"Or psychosis," he muttered. The words could have stung, but he offered them up with an easy familiarity. He and Emily had been having this conversation for a good five years now. Since the night after she had died.

"I can't say it's good to see you," he lied, glancing toward the bartender, who was shelving glasses and sniffing like he was fresh from Colombia. It was good to see her, everything considered. She was just as beautiful as she had ever been, just as funny. It made him miss her even more, her showing up every third day.

"*You're such a sweet talker,*" she said, breaking into a grin. "*You knew I'd be here: that's why you started in with the whiskey rather than popping another handful of pills. Think you're getting some sleep tonight?*"

"God willin' and the creek don't rise," he said, taking another swallow. "She'll be here."

She made a production of looking around the empty bar. "*I dunno, Tom. The prospects for a Jolene here . . . they're not filling me with a whole lot of optimism.*"

"She'll be here," he stressed. "There's always a Jolene."

"What?" The bartender asked from a few feet away.

"Nothin'." Tom waved it away. "Just goin' over the set list in my mind."

"You gonna do 'Jolene' tonight?" the kid asked, upping him considerably in Tom's esteem.

"God willin' and the creek don't rise," he repeated, slinging his feet over the empty chair beside him, leaning back to take a hearty swallow of bourbon straight from the bottle.

{

Jolene.

She had come by the merchandise table after the show at the Creekside Tavern. She waited for most of the line to clear out before she approached him. Always a good sign.

"Mister Chesnutt." She was bubbling over, her hair damp from dancing and sticking to her pale, pretty face. Her body was swaying to some internal music as she spoke. "I just wanted to tell you how much I loved the show tonight." She pushed a CD across the table toward him, and he uncapped his marker.

"Well thank you for sayin' that," he responded, laying on the country charm extra thick. "And you can call me Tom." She smiled and he fumbled with the CD booklet. Usually he just scrawled his name on the hard plastic shell, but when he wanted to spend a little extra time, he went for the booklet.

He glanced up, did a quick surveil: Emily was at the bar across the room, keeping company with a couple of good ol' boys.

He paused with his pen over his picture on the CD sleeve. "And what shall I call you, darlin'?"

There was a beat, a moment's silence. "Call me Jolene," she said.

He raised his eyebrows. "Honey, that song was a hit before your mama was born," he said as he autographed her CD and slid it back across the table toward her.

"Almost," she said, with a twinkle and a smile he could feel in his stomach.

"Now, Jolene . . ." He glanced up at Emily, safe out of earshot, as he spoke. "What say you stick around for a bit? Maybe we can have a drink once this place clears out some."

She didn't answer, but the smile she gave as she turned away said more than enough.

❧

From "The Weary Warrior of the Road," Monday Magazine:

Chesnutt won't discuss the mental breakdown which resulted in his forced hospitalization following Grace's death. "I think I've said enough about that for a lifetime," he says with a chuckle.

The accident and the hospital stay resulted in *Emily's Song*, the legendary album that has kept Chesnutt on the road since its release more than four years ago. "I don't even know if I have a house anymore," he laughs. "The mortgage payments keep coming out of the bank, but the place could have blown away for all I know." The singer hasn't been to his Spokane-area home more than a few nights since Grace's death. "It's too hard," he says. "There's really nothing for me there. Not anymore."

❧

No one really notices when he takes the stage. The room isn't full: lots of people outside smoking, hanging out, enjoying the cool summer evening breeze off the water. He's got no use for introductions, so when he picks up his Martin, people think he's a roadie or a guitar tech.

Without any sort of fanfare, with the houselights still up, he starts to tap the body of the guitar just above the strings. Tap tap. Tap tap. Two fingers, nice and soft.

People start to turn toward the stage as the sound carries out to them. The band is standing at the side of the stage, waiting.

He loves this part, the way the evening starts to take shape. It's one of the few things he still loves, these days.

Tap tap. Tap tap.

Over the speakers, over the monitors, the tapping sounds like a heartbeat.

Tap tap.

Somebody whoops. Nice to know somebody's buying the records.

Tap tap.

Eyes closed, he leans into the microphone, whispers the word "Jolene" and the place crackles with a sudden electricity. People come to their feet, crowding to the stage. As he sings the first words of the song, just the name, over and over, in a whisper, the band files in behind him.

Tap tap.

And just as the first chorus comes around, he turns to Frank and nods. The drummer kicks into "Right Child" and the band is right with him, right on the money. Smooth as an old dollar. Smooth as a well-told lie.

༆

From www.thewebmusicguide.com:

Tom Chesnutt—Live at Slim's

This album does little more than capture another night on the road for wandering troubadour Chesnutt and his crack band. It is anything but perfunctory, however. From a haunting, acapella opener of Dolly Parton's "Jolene," a harrowing set drawn largely from *Emily's Song*, through an intense, full-band encore of "Jolene" again, this is a transfixing set. Chesnutt sounds like a man possessed. Despite his well-deserved reputation as a songwriter, Chesnutt gets good mileage from several well-chosen covers, including a countrified stomp through the Rolling Stones' "19th Nervous Breakdown" (which Chesnutt introduces with a meandering story about time spent in a mental institution, finishing "And when you're faced with a two-hundred and fifty pound coloured orderly with a sixteen inch needle in his hand, the last thing you wanna say is 'Yeah? And what are you gonna do about it?'") Conspicuous by its absence is the title track from *Emily's Song*: Chesnutt, despite his near-constant touring, has never performed the song live.

(

He caught a couple of glimpses of her during the set.

His eye was drawn to her. He followed her as best he could through the night.

"You always liked that type," Emily whispered in his ear.

It wasn't until the encores, until the second run through "Jolene," that he was sure.

It was almost a Bo Diddley beat, and he could feel it in his sternum as he took the microphone and started to sing. He poured all of himself into the words, and fed off the sound of the crowd singing along.

When he hit the first note on the guitar, the place exploded, and he rode the crowd like a wave. There was no longer any resemblance to the pretty song that Miss Parton sang. This was more like Crazy Horse, a shuffling stomp that they'd still be feeling in their ears come morning.

The crowd bounced in place, punched the air, their faces contorted as they struggled to hear their own singing over the band.

She worked her way to the front, dancing by herself, holding her hands over her head. She moved with an easy, slow grace, a movement of her body that let anyone watching know that she knew how to move it.

Tom was watching.

"She's just your type, isn't she?"

With a single motion of his hand he brought the band down for the bridge, Frank tapping lightly on the snare, Billy walking the bass.

He stepped toward the microphone and whispered her name into it.

The crowd roared back

The redhead in front looked at him.

"Jolene." A little louder.

He let his eyes close, focussing all his energy on the name, on the sound of it on his lips. He repeated it over and over like a prayer, building gradually from a whisper to a full-throated roar, the energy of the crowd buoying him up, all that energy, all that passion, focussed on a single name.

"Jolene!"

The band kicked back in as he opened his eyes. All he could see was her, the pretty redhead in the front row, the one who had been dancing by herself but now just stood, staring at him.

He met her eyes, and she smiled.

"There's always a Jolene," Emily Grace whispered.

{

From The Daily Record (TV transcript):

Interviewer: It's been five years since the tragic death of your fianceé, Emily Grace. Has it been difficult to move on?

Chesnutt: I do nothin' but move on. Every night a different town.

Interviewer: But are you able to put that tragedy behind you?

Chesnutt: That's not how it works. I carry her with me. Everywhere I go, Emily Grace is right there with me.

{

After the show, the sound of the crowd still echoing, Tom stepped out the back door of the bar, wedging the fire exit open behind him.

His hands were shaking as he lit a cigarette with the Zippo

Emily had given him, but it was pure adrenaline. Not the drugs, just the rush of the show.

"Those things are gonna kill you," Emily said.

She was standing in the alley, looking up at him on the stoop.

He shrugged and took a heavy drag. "Lots of things that might kill me first."

"Most of them self-inflicted."

"Funny thing about that. Not a whole lot of things are self-inflicted if you look back far enough."

"Very profound, Tom. Are you trying to impress me, or just warming up for that pretty girl waiting for you inside?"

"Just feelin' good. It was a good show tonight."

She took the steps up to the stoop, laid her hand gently on his cheek. He wished he could feel it. Wished he could touch her again, even just once.

One more for the road.

"Don't sell yourself short, Tom. You always put on a good show."

He took another drag off his cigarette, listening to the crackling of the paper as it burned. "I can't tell if that was a compliment or just you bein' mean."

"Oh, Tom. I think we both know the answer to that question."

He chuckled.

"You tired, Tom?"

He hadn't noticed it. In the rush after the show, he felt light, almost weightless, vibrating like a plucked string. As soon as she asked, though, the weight of his exhaustion crashed in on him. His knees almost buckled under the weight.

He nodded. "It's been a couple of nights."

"I know it has, lover. How're you holding out?"

He took a last drag, ground out the butt under his boot heel. "I'm all right." Thinking about the pretty redhead, about what would happen later, the mix of guilt and anticipation turning in his stomach.

"That's funny. 'Cause from here, you look like ten pounds of shit in a five pound sack."

They both laughed at that.

"Tonight might be your night, though. That girl had nothin' but you in her eyes."

He nodded, his head heavy, spilling over with regret for things he hadn't done. Yet.

"You'd better get back in, Tom. Don't want to keep your public waiting."

❧

From www.thewebmusicguide.com (excerpt):

Tom Chesnutt—*Emily's Song* (Spoke Cane Records)

Fittingly, the emotional centrepiece of the album is the title track. As achingly personal and immediate as Neil Young's "Borrowed Tune," or Tori Amos' "Me and A Gun," "Emily's Song" is six minutes of unalloyed pain and loss, set to a forlorn acoustic guitar. This is the sound of a heart breaking, the midnight blues of Tom Chesnutt's dark night of the soul.

❧

"Thanks for comin' out," he said as he passed the signed CD back to the middle-aged man across the table.

"Do you say the same thing to everyone?" the pretty redhead asked, picking a CD off the table and pretending to look at the tracklist.

She had waited over by the bar, keeping her eye on the line, gliding over when there were just a couple of people left.

"That wouldn't be very much fun, would it?"

"I suppose not."

"Jolene," Emily whispered.

She was pretty, but not the kind of pretty that would necessarily catch most men's eyes. Her curly red hair was short above her shoulders, framing a roundish face. She wasn't tall, but she was curvy in all the right places, wearing a green sundress. Tom could see the straps of a red bra at her shoulders.

She nodded slowly as she pretended to read, the sparkle in her eye a dead giveaway that she knew he was looking.

"I'll take this one."

"Good choice."

"I bet you say that to all the girls."

"You'd win that bet." He fumbled with the booklet. "And who's this for?"

"Me," she said.

He leaned back in his chair and raised his eyebrows.

"Collette," she added, blushing a little. "I'm Collette."

Jolene.

That blush was the prettiest thing Tom had seen in days.

When he looked up again, she was fumbling with her wallet. He shook his head, waved away the twenty she held out to him. "Nah. Let's not worry about that." He handed the CD to her, making sure their fingers touched. "This is my gift to you. Because you waited so long in line, and I hate to keep a pretty lady waiting."

There was that blush again. He could feel it down to his toes.

"Well thank you, Mr. Chesnutt," she said, genuinely surprised.

"Just don't call me Mr. Chesnutt," he said. "That's all I ask."

"All right, Tom." She stressed his name, drawing it out a little, finishing with a little giggle that made him feel like he might just spontaneously combust.

"That's better."

"Listen, Tom—" she leaned into the table "—can I make you a drink?"

He looked away from the low neckline of her dress, down to his nearly empty glass of bourbon. "Well, they're taking pretty good care of me. . . ."

"No." She shook her head. "I was thinking I could make you a drink at my place."

Tom waited a beat before he even acknowledged having heard her. In that moment, he could see what asking had cost her. She wasn't the sort that came to every show to hit town, notches in her bedpost or whatever. When she made the offer, she had put herself out there. And here he was, letting her dangle.

"That'd be very kind," he said slowly, looking up at her. "Fella works up a hell of a thirst doing what I do."

As she smiled, she seemed to sag a little. Relief, he thought.

She'd been holding herself tight, waiting for him to answer. "I've got a car, if . . ."

He nodded. "Sure. Listen—" He leaned across the table, and she leaned in to meet him and he could smell the sweat, shampoo, boozy smell of her and it made his head swim.

He waited another beat, until she said, "Yeah?" This time, her voice was playful, flirtatious, and her lips seemed to linger on the single word.

"Do you mind if I bring my guitar?"

{

From KWAS Television, The News at Five:

Voiceover: Investigators now believe the car was driven by Spokane resident Emily Grace, who apparently was en route to Moses Lake early this morning when her vehicle left the road and plunged down the embankment. Investigators aren't confirming, but alcohol is believed to have been a factor. . . .

{

"I thought I'd take a longer route home," Collette said, a little nervously. "Show you a bit of the city."

"That sounds fine." His guitar case was in the back, Emily sitting beside it. Tom was slumped in the passenger seat, watching the lights passing by in blurry streaks of gold, watching her drive. If he kept his head angled just right, he didn't have to see Emily at all.

"Is there anything you want to listen to?" she asked, flipping down the visor to reveal a CD holder.

"Nope. Anything's good. So long as it's not me." He chuckled.

"You like Nina Simone?"

"Sure."

There were a few moments of small club applause before the music started.

She mouthed some of the words as Nina sang; it made Tom smile.

"*Just your type, isn't she?*"

"So are you from here?" he asked.

"Nah. Nobody's *from* Victoria. Everybody just ends up here."

"So where did you start out?"

"A little town you've probably never heard of. Henderson? On the mainland. You don't have to pretend like you know where it is; most people have never heard of it."

"Small-town girl."

"Farm girl," she corrected him. "My family grew corn, raised beef cattle."

"Sounds like where I grew up."

She nodded. "A lot smaller, though."

He got lost in the way the streetlights fell across her pale skin, the regular flashes of beauty, of softness. He realized that he was drunk, in that comfortable place where you're warm, where the world is filled with beauty, where every word has meaning.

"*You're feeling pretty good right now, aren't you?*" Emily asked.

"I was actually in Spokane for a little while."

He pulled himself together enough to respond. "What brought a girl like you to a place like Spokane?"

"I came for the waters," she said, glancing at him to see if he caught the reference.

"You were misinformed," he said, playing along.

"That I was," she said, shaking her head.

"So it was a man?"

"Isn't it always?"

He shook his head ruefully. "The things we do. . . ."

"I was supposed to marry him."

"Really?"

She nodded. "I was young. Dumb. In love. I met this cowboy and he swept me off my feet."

"They do that."

"Yeah. Anyways, this was almost six years ago now, I guess. I fell madly in love. Would have followed my cowboy anywhere. Ended up following him to Spokane."

"That'll learn ya."

"Yeah."

She drove in silence for a few moments.

"So did you marry your cowboy?"

"No, I got wise. He introduced me to some of his friends. And their wives. And they were all sweet men, and their wives were lovely. Beautiful and kind. But they all had this look in their eyes, this caged, sort of desperate look. Trapped and they knew they could never admit it."

"Sounds familiar."

"That was enough for me. I broke that cowboy's heart, ended up here."

As she said the words, she turned the car into the driveway of a rambling three-storey house, killed the engine.

"This place yours?"

"The second floor is. My landlady has the bottom floor, and a friend has the attic. You'd like the place. Full of artists." She started to open her door.

He shook his head. "I don't know. I don't hold much truck with artists." He waited a beat. "What do you do?"

She leaned back into the car. "I'm a waitress."

He smiled and opened his door. "I get along with waitresses just fine."

⸙

From KWAS Television, The News At Five:

Voiceover: Spokane Police are reporting that this afternoon's standoff at a downtown bar ended peacefully when country singer Tom Chesnutt surrendered himself to police a few minutes ago. Chesnutt reportedly entered the Creekside Tavern at shortly after one this afternoon with a loaded firearm. A police spokesman says they are not regarding this incident as a hostage-taking.

Interview: Mister Chesnutt made no threats to the staff or clientele of the business. According to eyewitnesses, he was visibly upset, and threatened to take his own life.

Voiceover: Speculation is that this afternoon's incident is related to the death of Mr. Chesnutt's fiancée Emily Grace in a car accident earlier this week. Mr. Chesnutt has been taken to a mental health facility for observation. . . .

(

"Can I get you that drink?" Collette asked as she pushed the door closed behind them.

"No matter how many times you hear them, those words are like music."

She dropped her purse on the couch, looked back at him over her shoulder in a way that made his stomach drop. "Bourbon, right? Maker's Mark okay?"

"That'll do just fine." He leaned his guitar case against a battered armchair, covered with an old quilt.

"You want anything fancy?"

"An ice cube?"

"I think I can manage that."

As she went into the kitchen he looked around the room.

She had done her best to keep the place homey, with tapestries and batiks on the walls, a couple of small tables with vintage lamps, a battered couch to match the battered chair. The air smelled faintly of incense and pot smoke. He didn't see a TV anywhere, but her stereo . . .

He had to get up to get a closer look.

"This is a nice rig," he said when he heard her feet patting across the floor. She had taken offer her shoes: the sound of bare feet on hardwood. . . .

She pressed the drink into his hand. "Did I get it right?"

He took a swallow as if to test it out. "That tastes just fine." He clinked his glass against hers.

She turned to the stereo. "It was my father's," she explained.

"And he left it to you?"

She choked back a chuckle. "No, he upgraded. He likes his toys and he likes them new." She shrugged. "It works out well for me."

He picked up the record sleeve that had been leaning against the amplifier, looked at the picture of himself in full flight at Slim's. "So you're the one."

She looked at him quizzically.

"The one who keeps buying vinyl."

"Nothing else like it."

He sat in the chair, and she settled on the couch across the coffee table from him, next to Emily Grace, who just stared at him without blinking.

"You're in fine form tonight," Emily said.

Collette took another sip from her drink.

"So which guitar did you bring?"

He glanced at the case beside the chair. "My old J-45. Best guitar ever made. I bought it to celebrate my first record deal."

She nodded appreciatively. "Nice." Another sip. "Does it play?"

"Not by itself." He laid the case on his lap, lifted out the Gibson. "Time to sing for my supper, I guess." He played his fingers across the strings, tightened a couple of the keys so little he might not have done anything at all—he could hear the difference, though.

"Any requests?" he joked.

"Do you know 'Freebird?'" she asked, not missing a beat.

He chuckled, plucked out the first couple of notes.

"Should I get my lighter?" she asked, with a playful grin. Her lips glistened, thick and wet in the dim light.

He smiled, nodded at the joke, then asked, "Now that you mention it, though: do you mind if I smoke?"

She shook her head. "I'll just . . ." She bustled around, cracking open a window, bringing him an ashtray. He watched every movement, every breath.

"You like this one, don't you?"

He sighed, dug his pack of Lucky Strikes out of his pocket.

"But you like all of them, don't you, Tom? That's the problem."

"That should do," she said, returning to the couch.

"Thanks. I 'preciate that." He lit the cigarette and took a deep, hot drag.

"I'm gonna play you a song—" she had a smile that could light up the darkest of hearts "—that I don't . . . I've never played this for anyone. It's got a story that goes with it, though. I'll tell you the story first, then you can let me know if you still want to hear the song."

He rested the smoke in the ashtray, took a long swallow and set his drink down next to it.

Collette leaned forward on the couch; Emily leaned back. They both stared at him.

What's the worst thing you can imagine, Tom? The worst punishment someone could wish on you?

"I've been doing this a long time," he started, not looking at either of them, staring into the woodgrain of the guitar's face as the well-practiced patter started to come out of him. "I've travelled a lot of miles, sung a lot of songs, met a lot of women." He smiled, let his eyes connect with Collette's, then looked away.

"But there's only one woman I've ever loved. Only one woman I'm ever likely to love."

"Emily Grace," Collette whispered, and hearing her name in the girl's voice gave him a chill right to the heart.

"I loved her. Not well. And I lost her."

"I was there," Collette said quietly.

"What?" He wasn't used to being interrupted, not at that part of the story. It threw him.

"I was there. In Spokane. When Emily died. When you . . ." Her voice trailed off. "That was when I was in Spokane, not getting married to my cowboy."

"*Seems you've got yourself a ringer,*" Emily said, smiling.

"I watched it all on the news. I always wondered—"

"There's a lot you don't hear on the news. A lot of half-told stories. This is . . . this is the whole truth—"

"*Oh, honey.*"

"—the only way I can tell it."

She nodded, her eyes wide.

"I loved her. And I lost her. And it was all my fault."

He took a long drink from the tumbler. His hand was shaking again.

"I met Emily Grace when I was twenty-seven or twenty-eight. I say we met then, but she'd always been around. One of those people you see around, but you never really notice."

"Thanks."

"But we met. She was twenty, I guess. We fell in love, got a place together, this shitty little walk-up. I made my music. She waited tables."

Collette bowed her head.

"We were happy. We had no money, not a pot to piss in, but we had each other. We were happy."

"We were."

"But I was a road dog. I was on tour a lot in those days. Not as much as I am now." He barked out a laugh. "But a lot. Away from home. Away from her. In the path of vice and degradation. Opportunity, I liked to call it."

"Dogging, I used to call it."

"See, I love women. I love all women. Always have. I love the way they look, the way they smell, the way they feel." He looked at Collette, then shook his head, trying to clear off the reverie.

"I was in love with Emily, but . . ." He shrugged.

"You were incorrigible."

"Incorrigible. That's a good word."

"That's a good word for it. The road's a hard place if you're trying to stay true. And I didn't even try. I slept with a lot of women, but, I don't know how, in my heart I stayed true."

"Did she know?"

"Yes."

"Maybe. It was something we joked about: me and my groupies. But we didn't ever really talk about it."

"What happens on the road stays on the road."

"Something like that, yeah."

She nodded slowly, like she was trying to figure out her place in all of this.

"I carved up a lot of road in my younger days."

"A lot of notches in your guitar strap."

He grinned. "Yeah."

The bourbon went down just fine, thank you very much.

"When I was first together with Emily, I managed to stop, though."

"For a while."

"For a while. But a pretty girl is hard to resist."

She blushed again, and Tom had to look away.

"We were happy. When I wasn't on the road, we spent all our time together. We got engaged. Bought a house. Started talking about how it might work to have a family. We were together for more than ten years."

"And then she died."

He shook his head. "Don't get ahead of me now, darling."

"Sorry."

"Round about six years ago now—"

"You know exactly how long it's been."

"—I was doing some local shows. Road-testing some songs I was working on. I played one night at the Creekside Tavern. That's where I met her."

"Jolene."

"She called herself Jolene."

"That's not your real name, is it?" he had asked her, after, his arm around her shoulders, her head nestled on his chest.

"You'll never know," she whispered, still playing.

He smoothed the hair away from her face.

"Like the song."

"Yeah. She came up to me after the show. Waited until she was the last person at the merch table."

Collette looked down at the floor.

"I asked her if she wanted to stay around for a while. Maybe have a drink. She did."

"Of course she did," Emily said.

"Of course she did," Collette said quietly, staring a hole into the hardwood.

"I had her wait for me at the bar. The other end of the bar from where Emily was sitting."

"Emily was there?"

"I'm always there."

He nodded. "She'd been there all night. Listening to the new songs. Standin' by her man. When she asked if I was all done, if I was ready to go home. I told her—" he took a deep breath "—I told her that I was headed out for Moses Lake with the band. We had a show there the next night. I made it sound like this had always been the plan, that she and I had talked about it, that she'd forgotten. . . ."

"Bastard."

"And the whole time I was spinnin' her this line, I could see Jolene at the far end of the bar, looking at me over Emily's shoulder, this little smile on her face as I was lying to the woman I loved, trying to get rid of her."

He lit another cigarette, hands shaking something fierce now.

"Emily was confused, I guess. A little drunk. She had no idea what I was talking about, but she ordered us another couple of drinks—"

"One for the road."

"—and we drank and she gave me a kiss goodbye and told me to behave myself. Told me she loved me. And the moment she was gone, Jolene up and took her place at the bar.

"I expected Emily to go home. It never occurred to me that she'd head out to Moses Lake as well. But she talked to Frank as she was leaving, found out what hotel they were staying at without letting on that she thought I was coming with them. And then she went home, packed a toothbrush and whatnot, and headed out to surprise me."

"Jesus," Collette whispered.

"Yeah. I figure it must have been about the same time I was, well, I figure it was about the same time I was back at Jolene's that she lost control of the car—"

"One more for the road, baby."

"—and went over that embankment. Police said it looked like maybe she fell asleep. That she probably didn't feel anything."

He looked at Emily for some comment, some sign that the police were right, that she hadn't suffered, but she just stared him cold.

"I killed her," he said, plain and true. "I killed her as sure as if I put a bullet in her. I killed her because I couldn't resist a pretty girl." He shook his head, waiting for Collette to contradict him. Waited in vain. "If it wasn't for me, she wouldn't have been out there on the road that night. If it wasn't for me—"

"She'd still be alive."

"Smart girl."

He took a deep drag off the cigarette then balanced it on the ashtray, folding his arms around his guitar and hugging it to himself.

"But that's only part of it."

Collette's eyes were wide, and Emily leaned forward on the couch, watching him watching her.

"I spent the night with that girl. Let her make me breakfast. And then I went home to pick up some clothes and such for the night in Moses Lake. She was supposed to be at work. The car wasn't in the driveway. But when I got inside, Emily Grace was waiting for me."

❧

She was wearing the same thing she had been wearing in the bar, sitting on the couch in a slant of sunshine. She looked at him as he came through the door, but she didn't make any move to get up. Just looked at him.

"Did you have a good time, lover?" she asked, and his heart dropped between his boots. Busted. "Did you have a good time? I hope she was worth it."

He started to argue, tried to make excuses, come up with some story, but she just shook her head. Then she asked, "Tom, what's your worst nightmare? What's the worst thing you can imagine?"

The question came out of nowhere, and as he tried to answer, there was a knocking at the door.

"You're gonna wanna get that," she said.

♪

"It was Highway Patrol, come to tell me that Emily Grace had died. I tried to tell them they were wrong, but when I looked back, she was gone."

Collette was no longer even trying to meet his eye.

"I thought I was going crazy. I *did* go crazy. You were there, you remember how hot it was that week: I couldn't sleep, I couldn't eat, I couldn't cry. The police, they showed me pictures of the wreck, pictures of her. I couldn't hold it together. That first day I must have drunk my way through two bottles of bourbon trying to ignore the phone, trying to put her out of my mind. It didn't work. I was wide awake, sober as a judge, when she walked into our room that night."

♪

The red numbers on the clock radio read 3:11. He didn't hear anything, but he could feel her there, knew she was with him.

"Emily?" he said.

She sat down next to him, but there was no weight to shift the balance of the bed. She leaned over him, close to his ear. He was hoping for words of comfort, something to let him sleep.

Instead, she sang in a whisper, words from an old Leadbelly song. "*My boy, my boy, don't you lie to me, tell me where did you sleep last night?*"

She disappeared before he could answer.

ᘓ

"The next day was the same. More booze. People coming to the house, but I pretended I wasn't home. That night, though—" He nodded heavily. "That night I cried. I bawled like a baby, for everything I had done, for everything I had lost. I cried like a child, and when she came to me, she took one look, shook her head, and disappeared. The next day . . . Have you ever gone three days without sleep?"

Collette thought for a moment, then shook her head.

"It's rough at the best of times. Your mind starts to play tricks on you, talking nonsense, but making it sound like wisdom. So it made perfect sense to me to take my daddy's gun and head back to the Creekside. Scene of the crime. I thought . . . I figured I'd end it all. Put myself out of my misery. People thought I wanted to kill myself so I could be with her. Truth is, I wanted to kill myself so I wouldn't have to see her, ever again."

"Funny how things work out," Emily said.

"It's funny how things work out. She was there, sitting at the bar like she was the last time I saw her. And I pulled out that gun and I put the barrel in my mouth, I had my finger on the trigger, and she leaned in, she leaned in real close, and she said, 'You can't do it, can you? All your big hat, big balls posturing, and you can't even muster up the guts to take the cowardly way out.' And then she asked me again, 'What's your worst nightmare, Tom?' but this time, she had the answer."

ᘓ

He had lowered the gun as she stepped toward him, letting it dangle at his hip.

"I'm gonna tell you what your life is gonna look like, Tom," she said, in the same reedy voice she had once used to say she loved him. "You're not gonna sleep. You'll barely eat. You'll be so close to snapping all the time, you'll feel like a rubber band." The words didn't sound like a threat or a curse, just a description of the way things were gonna be. "And the only thing that'll help you, the only way you'll have to find some peace, to find some rest, is gonna be to tell your story. To find someone, and tell them what you've done."

"'Rime of the Ancient Mariner,'" Collette whispered.

"She's brighter than most."

Tom nodded. "Yeah."

"So that's . . . why me? Why'd you pick me?" He could see the distaste forming on her face, the blossoming sense of betrayal. That's what it looks like when you realize you've been used.

Tom had to look away. "Because you wanted to listen. Because it's been three nights since I last told anyone. Three days since I slept. Because I get so tired. . . ."

"Tell her. You have to tell her."

"Because you're Jolene," he said, and the words felt like they might break him, same as they always did.

The look of horror on her face was the same, too. How many times had he seen that? Too many.

"There's one in every crowd: the girl who waits 'til the end of the line. The girl with the secret smile. The girl who I can feel right down to my toes."

He shook his head.

"The sort of girl I'd do it all for again, if the circumstances were the same."

Collette gasped, and Emily smiled, and Tom just went on talking. "The girl who helped me kill her, and didn't even know. That's what she wants—she wants you to know. Emily wants you to know what you've done. She wants you to know what it's in you to do."

She looked at him for a long moment, tears streaming down her cheeks, betrayal working hard in her eyes, and then she crumpled, her back jumping as she cried. Emily looked at her for a moment, looked at Tom, then vanished, as if she'd never been there at all.

He thought, for a passing moment, that he might go over to Collette, rub her back, try to comfort her. He liked this girl; he didn't like to see her in pain. In pain that he had caused.

But that was the point, wasn't it?

Instead, he put his guitar back in its case, unplayed and forlorn, his song unheard for another night. His cigarette had burned itself out, leaving a white column of ash.

He didn't say anything as he left—there was nothing he could say—but he looked back at her, thinking wishes and might-have-beens.

He closed the door behind himself. Heard it lock.

The sound of his boot heels on the sidewalk echoed in the empty night. Behind him, the road stretched on forever, disappearing into the sea and the dark sky beyond. Ahead, just ahead, a hotel. A bed. A night of broken sleep, from which he would wake sadder but no wiser.

And tomorrow . . .

The weight of his guitar case was almost too much to bear. He wondered, as he walked in line with the journeying moon, when, if ever, he might have the guts to put it down, once and for all.

CROSSROADS BLUES

I sold my soul to the devil in the parking lot of a 7-Eleven.

I wish it had been at a crossroads, you know? Or in a graveyard. Or, hell, anywhere cooler than a fucking convenience store parking lot. Just for colour, you know?

Because we've all heard the story. Hell, everyone who's ever dreamt of bending that note, or writing that one perfect song, we've all thought about it. Go down to the crossroads like Robert Johnson did, sell your soul and come back with your touch, your sound, your songs.

Sure, he died young and barking like a dog. But have you ever heard "Love in Vain?" "Crossroads Blues?" "Hellhounds on my Trail?" Hear songs like that, and you realize that how he ended up didn't matter. The songs are all that matter.

You'd sell your soul to write a song half that good.

At least, that's what you tell yourself.

Just to be clear—nobody expects it to happen, right? It's just a story, a fantasy when you're practicing so hard your fingers are bleeding. It's not real.

All the same, that afternoon, out front of the 7-Eleven? I knew who he was before he even opened his mouth.

He just—he looked the part, you know? Tall and skinny, dressed in black head to toe, with this long black coat that seemed to billow in the wind even though there was no wind. Short black hair. Good shoes. Expensive shoes. And me looking like shit, sitting on the ground by the door, my guitar case in front of me. I'd seeded it with a few coins, a couple of dollar bills, and that's all there was in it.

What I remember most, though? He smiled. A lot. And it was this big, open smile. He was like the kind of guy you could see hanging out with, maybe having drinks every couple of weeks. He looked like the sort of guy who would be anybody's friend.

Which, I suppose, makes sense. Of course the devil's gonna be friendly. Of course you're gonna want to be friends with him. It's all in the marketing.

But I knew from the moment I saw him who he was. What it meant.

I had my head down, looking at my fingering, trying to figure out one of those Bob Dylan songs. They're bastards—they seem so fucking easy as you listen to them, but when you go to try to figure them out there's so much going on.

Anyway.

I was looking at my fingering, and when I looked up he was standing right in front of me, just watching me. I have no clue where he came from, he was just there. As soon as I saw that smile, that cat, I knew.

And you could tell that he knew that I knew. He smiled. Well, of course he did—me knowing? That just made it all so much easier.

"I'm impressed," he said, nodding slowly. The absence of any sort of accent was almost an accent in itself. "You've got a good touch."

I nodded, trying to play it cool. "Thanks."

"And a passable singing voice."

"I wasn't singing," I said. Fuck, the balls I must have had.

His smile got wider and I set my guitar in the case, started to my feet.

"Not then, no."

"Then how can you—"

"Oh please, Charles," he said, waving his hand. A cigarette appeared in it, and then he was lighting it with a Zippo in his other hand. "Let's not play games, shall we? You know who I am."

"I suppose you know everything about me," I said, still ballsy.

He let smoke drift out from between his lips. "Of course I do."

"Of course."

"For starters," and he pointed at my guitar with his cigarette. "I know just how badly you want to make something of that."

"What, you don't figure a guy dreams of sitting on the sidewalk outside a fucking 7-Eleven store, playing for change?"

"Or *not* playing for change, as the case might be."

"And I suppose you can help me out with that."

"Maybe," he said, flicking the cigarette away.

"I've heard the stories," I said. And you know, to this day I'm not sure how I mustered up the nuts. I mean, we're talking about the devil, for fuck's sake. But I was twenty—I thought I knew shit. "How you met Robert Johnson at the crossroads—"

"You shouldn't believe everything you hear," he said. "My reputation's taken a bit of a beating."

I bit back the snotty response I was going to make.

"So," he said, taking a step forward. "Do you want to be a rock and roll star?" He smiled so widely I could have counted his teeth.

And I said "Sure" like it was a foregone conclusion, like we were finally getting around to the heart of the matter after all the bullshit pleasantries had passed. Like when you're scoring at someone's house and you have to make fucking small talk before he pulls out the fucking scales.

He shook his head a little dismissively like, then he crouched down in front of my guitar case. "Nice guitar," he said, looking down into it. "Was it worth all those bullshit hours you had to put in to buy it?"

It took me a second, but I twigged: if he knew everything about me then he sure as shit knew about that summer I worked at the restaurant, hoarding my tips, watching every penny until I could afford the guitar in the music store window.

"Yeah. Definitely worth it."

He nodded, not taking his eyes off it. And then he reached out and he just touched it, ran his finger up the neck.

Nothing more than that.

Then he stood up, straightened his coat.

"Well," he said, and I felt like I might burst from anticipation.

And he started to turn away. "Good luck with it," he said.

"Wait," I said, taking a step toward him. "That's it?"

He stopped and turned back. "That's what?"

That stopped me for a moment. I thought we were both talking about the same thing. "That's all it takes? You touch my guitar and walk away?"

"All what takes?" he asked, like I was speaking a foreign language.

"That stuff . . ." I didn't know how to put it. "All that stuff about me being a star. How does that work?"

He grinned, this big shit-eating grin. "Practice. Practice. Practice," he said slowly, like butter wouldn't melt in his mouth. I wanted to punch him in the smug, fucking face. "I'll be seeing you, Charlie Webber."

And that time, he turned and walked away.

I looked down at my guitar, but I knew I wasn't going to be busking any more that day. Not after that. Hell, I figured my busking days were behind me. I'd made my deal; it was time to start collecting.

I snapped the case shut and headed for home. I got there just as Desiree was waking up, and I crawled back into bed with her. She was late for her shift at the restaurant but her boss was trying so hard to get into her pants she could have taken a shit in the soup and she'd have been fine.

I didn't touch my guitar that night. I left the case standing in the corner, and I smoked a couple of joints and listened to some records: Clapton and the Allmans and the Dead. I wasn't scared or anything. I wasn't trying to psych myself up. I just wanted to be ready, you know?

The next morning, though?

Jesus.

The next day, everything changed. I picked up my guitar and it just felt different, you know? I can't really describe it, but it was like my whole relationship with it had changed. After I'd been playing for a while, after I was nice and loose, I decided to stretch a bit, test myself, see what I had gotten myself into. And that guitar sang. I was playing, really pushing myself, and it felt like I couldn't hit a bum note.

So I just played for a while, seeing what I could do, and I hit this riff and I knew: it was gold. I mean, it was fucking "Satisfaction" gold, you know? You hear it and you're like "Fuck, this is something else."

Well, this was something else.

And then just as easy the words started to come. I had to run around like a headless fucking chicken to find paper and a pen and I kept repeating the verses in my head until I found them.

My first song.

I could have kissed that old devil.

I kept it up for who knows how long. I got lost in it. And when I came out it was after dark. I vaguely recalled Desiree leaving for work, but it hadn't really registered with me.

I threw on a different shirt, grabbed my guitar, and headed down to the Marquee. Phil Astley and his boys were playing—it was a Monday night and they always played Monday nights—and he had told me that if I ever wanted to sit in I was more than welcome.

I had never done it—fuck, Phil and the boys were pros and I had no interest in stinking up the stage, but I knew I couldn't lose now.

And I didn't.

Phil seemed a bit surprised to see me, but he was cool about it. He took one look at my guitar and shook his head and gave me an electric. And Jesus, that was the night, man. That was the first night of the rest of my life.

I don't remember what we played—it was all covers back then— but I remember how it felt, bending those notes, hearing my voice in the monitors. I got a blowjob from this chick in the men's room, but the best part of the night, the best part, was when Phil looked over at me while I was playing with this look on his face, and I was all like "Yeah, motherfucker, this is what a star looks like."

After that, I was in the band. We started doing things differently. Phil and I were both writing songs and we took turns at the mic. People started coming out to see us because we were something new, something different. We weren't just some fucking bar band, we had some depth. Our own songs. Two singers. Two guitar players.

We started opening shows on big tours. Theatres and arenas

all through the west. Phil had this fucking manager—Bill? Was that his name? He didn't last long once I was in the band, once we started getting real gigs. Man, he'd have had us playing the Marquee every Monday night until we got old and dried up if he'd had his way. Andy, our new manager? He knew we were headed straight to the fucking top.

Phil didn't last long either. The record company guy told me— just between us—that the band would be better off if there was just one focal point, just one set of pipes. Phil was holding us back, and me and the guys, we didn't want to be held back. We were on tour, opening for—fuck, I can't even remember—and we had a band meeting one night before Phil got there, and we let him know that he could play out the last few shows with us, he was . . .

Well, you know. The rest is history.

Me and the band made that first record, but it wasn't the same, so I had to get rid of the rest of the band too. We had to scramble, because Andy had us a tour booked, but it all worked out. Charlie Webber. My name up in lights.

That first record was huge. Well, I guess you know that. And I was completely overwhelmed. I mean, my dreams were coming true, right? I got lost in it. Deer in fucking headlights.

And then I got home and it was like running into a brick fucking wall. I went from Charlie fucking Webber to would you mind doing the laundry while I'm at work? I mean, are you fucking kidding me? I had songs to write, for fuck's sake.

I couldn't hack it, man. I told Desiree I was leaving, headed to L.A. to work on the next record and I wasn't coming back. I told her she could stay in the apartment for the rest of the month while she found somewhere else, but I'd given notice.

I was going to L.A.

I was already gone.

L.A.

L.A was a fucking dream come true. The record company put me up in a bungalow at the Chateau Marmont to write and it was a fucking party every night. You wouldn't believe it if I told you. I mean, the first time I did blow it was with—well, I probably shouldn't say. His estate isn't exactly too fond of these kinds of stories.

And the women. Man. Chicks will do anything for a singer. Especially if he plays a little guitar, too. Anything. Hell, if I didn't get my dick sucked before lunch, I was having a bad day. Those nights—man, I got into some fucked up shit, I gotta tell you.

But I was working hard, too. Work hard. Play hard. Fuck hard. Repeat. The second record, that was the one that broke us wide. Arenas all the way, headlining. Drugs. Chicks. Living the dream.

And it didn't stop. There was no fucking re-entry, man. I'd finish out a tour and figure out where I wanted to record next. Who I wanted to record with. It was amazing.

I'd like to say that I never thought about him, you know? I'd like to say that, after that afternoon out front of the 7-Eleven I'd never given him a second thought, but that'd be a lie. Truth is, not a day went by I didn't think about him, not a show that I didn't think, at least once, well, this one's for Old Nick. They were all for Old Nick.

So there were the records. And the shows. And the chicks. And the drugs.

Over time, I kind of built up a world around myself. It happens. You're in a different city every night or two, you can't really be expected to keep track of shit, you know? That's why I had Derek.

Andy had hired him—he'd worked with him before. His formal title was Road Manager, but his job was to take care of me.

Worth his weight in gold, Derek. And that's major—Derek was no tiny motherfucker. Huge. Built like a brick fucking shithouse.

He got me out of a lot of scrapes.

There was this one night—Buffalo? Toronto? Montreal? Boston? Fucked if I know. All I remember is it was cold. This must have been after the third or fourth record, I guess. God, it was a fucking gong show every night. After the concerts we'd have these parties, back at the hotel. Lots of chicks. Lots of drugs. Up all night. Falling into whoever you wanted, in whatever way you wanted.

Anyway.

This one night in Toronto or Buffalo or fucking wherever, there was this chick. Why can't I remember her name? Anyway, she was in one of the bedrooms, and after everyone cleared out, she was still there.

She wasn't going anywhere.

I don't know if it was bad coke or too much coke or smack or what, but she'd taken her last hit, if you know what I mean. I mean, I wasn't there when it happened, all right? I just found her, okay? I wasn't there when she died. But I freaked the fuck out. I mean, there was a dead seventeen-year-old in my bed, and drugs all over the fucking place—what was I supposed to do?

So I called Derek, and he showed up in like two minutes, and he took one look and he says to me, "Why don't you have a shower while I deal with our little situation here?"

So I went and had a shower and when I came out the girl was gone and the drugs were gone and he'd cleaned up all the puke. Motherfucker even made the bed.

I never asked him about it. I figured it was just one of those things, you know? And he never brought it up. Not even when he could have. When it could have saved him.

I feel like a total prick for what happened to him. But I wasn't in any shape. . . .

I mean, that's the thing, right?

You smoke a joint and you want to listen to records and have sex.

You do a little blow, you want to play a show and get your dick sucked and do some more blow.

You start doing smack, though? It's not too long before you don't give a shit about doing shows or about getting your dick sucked. It's better than that. So much better. You just want to do more smack. You need to. It's not even about getting high. It's just about . . . I don't even know how to describe it. It's just . . . doing smack.

You don't give a shit about anything else. You don't give a fuck about who used the works, or what they might have. And you sure don't give a fuck what happens when your road manager is arrested for possession and trafficking because he was mailing packages of heroin to himself from hotel to hotel so that you'd never have to go without, or figure out how to score in a strange city.

So yeah. I testified against him. I didn't have any choice. It was all Andy's idea anyway. He told me we'd get me clean so I could testify, and we'd make sure that Derek was taken care of once he got out of prison. So that's what I did. I got clean. I testified. And you know, he could have rolled on me. He could have told the story about me and that chick in Buffalo or wherever. He could have told the jury what really happened, and how I asked him to mail the heroin ahead to every city we were going to be playing in, but he didn't. He just fucking sat there and took it for the team. Didn't even flinch when the judge sentenced him to three years. He was a good friend. He didn't deserve to go like that, shivved and bleeding out in a fucking prison shower. He wouldn't have even been there if it wasn't for me.

But I guess nobody gets away with it forever, you know? Karma catches up. And it's a bitch.

I've been in rehab three times, but I've quit quitting each time. It just didn't stick. This time it did, though. It's hard to argue with a morphine drip, and let's face it, my chances of scoring in here are pretty fucking remote.

Hep C. The doctors tell me it's either from a dirty needle or somewhere I was putting my dick. Not like it fucking matters— I'm laying here waiting for a liver, but I know my chances are slim. I'm not a good candidate—I've done way too much damage to myself, so any liver that comes in they'll give it to some fucking soccer mom, two-and-a-half kids and a fucking mini-van.

And you know, they should. They totally fucking should. I'm the last person who deserves a second chance.

That's what I've come up with, laying here. I don't deserve a second chance. No, that's not it. I've had nothing *but* second chances, and I've fucked each and every one of them. So this is it. End of the line.

I got that message loud and clear, when Old Nick himself swanned into my room, coat billowing even though there's not the slightest fucking trace of a breeze.

"Hello, Charlie Webber," he said. "I heard you were feeling poorly." His smile reminded me of having the clap—just looking at him made me feel like I was pissing blood.

He hadn't changed a bit. Hadn't aged a day. Here I was, in a bed I was never going to leave, old before my time, ten pounds of shit in a five pound bag, and this cocksucker waltzes in, wearing that pretty-boy mask.

"You couldn't even wait, could you?" I said, still ballsy, to the end.

He came right up to the head of the bed. "Wait for what?"

"To collect on your end of the deal."

His smile bared his teeth. "What deal?"

I shook my head. "You fucker." All bravado, right? I mean, what did it matter now?

He shook his head right back. "Charlie, Charlie, Charlie," he said. "You really should have listened. You shouldn't believe everything you hear."

"What the fuck is that supposed to mean?"

He leaned against the edge of the bed. "Her name was Amber," he said. "The girl in Toronto. The girl you killed with the speedball. Remember her?"

I closed my eyes for a moment, finally nodding slowly, the bravado oozing out of me, leaving me flat.

"Yeah. Of course you do. Derek wrapped her body in the hotel sheets, and he dumped her in an alley near one of those cool hotels, you know the ones. Everybody figured that she scored in the club, went out into the alley to take her hit. They didn't look at it too closely. Why would they? She wasn't anyone. She didn't matter. Not to you. Not to anyone."

I thought of Amber, and of Derek. Of that night, and every night since.

"You cocksucker," I muttered weakly, trying to find some way to argue with him. "You did this."

"No, Charlie." He leaned in close, his face just inches from mine, and for a moment I thought he was going to kiss me. "You did this. This is what you wanted. This is where you were headed all along."

"But my guitar. You touched my guitar."

This time, he did laugh, and I've gotta tell you, that's a sound you never want to hear: the devil laughing at you. "And what? You thought I put a spell on it? You thought I'd given you some kind of gift?"

I was too embarrassed to respond—of course that's what I had thought.

"It was a beautiful guitar, Charlie. You'd worked very hard for it. I was just admiring it." He stood up and stepped away from the bed. "I wonder whatever happened to it."

It took a second, but then the full weight of everything crushed in on me. That guitar—it had meant so much to me. It had been my world, and I hadn't even thought of it in, fuck, decades. It was just gone. Just like so much else.

He had turned and was walking toward the door, but he stopped and looked back at me. I thought he just wanted to see me crying, broken. But no.

"Charlie, I'm gonna tell you a little secret. Are you ready?"

I didn't say anything.

"I didn't give you anything, Charlie. I didn't do anything for you. And most importantly? I didn't make you do anything. Free will, Charlie. Everything you did, everything you earned, every person you screwed over, you did all that on your own. You did it because you wanted to."

He leaned in close, and he spoke in almost a whisper. "I've never bought a soul," he said. "Ever. I've never made a deal." He straightened back up and looked like he was doing his best not to laugh. "Really. I know you don't believe me, but I've never made a deal. I've never needed to. Why buy a soul when you people are so eager to just give them away?"

He started walking slowly to the door. For a moment he looked almost sad. Almost human.

He looked back at me one last time from the doorway, and he smiled.

"I'll be seeing you."

BLESSING

Paul and Abigail realized, lying together on their wedding night, that they had never actually met.

Their families had lived on the same block, just outside the centre of Henderson, for their whole lives. They were the same age, had gone to the same school, went to the same church, and when it became apparent that there was no one else they would rather spend their lives with, both sets of their parents offered them the same blessing.

They were married in the spring of their twentieth year, in the United Church that they had always attended. It was filled with friends and family, grandparents, cousins, children playing noisily in the basement while the vows were taken, causing more than one smile in the congregation.

{

Before the wedding, over dinner at Abigail's parent's home, both sets of parents had insisted that two more people be added to the guest-list: John Joseph and his wife Claire.

It was impossible not to know John and Claire Joseph. They were an elderly couple who lived on a farm skirting the edge of the woods, where they grew enough for themselves, nothing left over even to sell in town at the Saturday market. They both still came in for the market, but they spent more time walking around and talking to whomever they encountered than they did shopping. It always seemed they went home empty-handed. And it was well-known in Henderson that they were among the wisest people around—that if there were a problem that needed solving, or a question that needed answering, sooner or later it would be asked to John or Claire Joseph.

It was in this light that Paul first saw the invitation. "Do we have a problem, Dad? Do we still need more counselling?" They had just finished a series of counselling sessions with the minister to prepare them for the wedding and the marriage afterward.

The two mothers smiled at one another, and shook their heads. "No, it's not that way at all," Paul's mother said.

"She was at both of our weddings," Paul's father said from the end of the table, taking a pull on his pipe.

"Every person married in town invites John and Claire to the wedding," Abigail's mother confirmed. "It's part of the compact."

Paul and Abigail looked at one another.

"The what?" Abigail asked.

"She wants to meet all the young people that she'll be seeing," Abigail's mother said delicately. "She's the . . . She helped in your birth, Abby." She laid her hand across the table, over her daughter's.

"And yours," Paul's mother added.

Both of the fathers just sat, watching, neither saying a word. Smoke from Paul's father's pipe curled toward the ceiling.

"Don't you remember them at Rob and Brenda's wedding last year?" Abigail's mother asked.

Rob and Brenda were friends of Paul and Abigail's, and their wedding the previous year was the first they had attended as adults. When Paul thought about it, he vaguely recalled Claire and John Joseph almost fading into the background in one of the rear pews.

"I guess," Paul said, still not entirely sure.

"But I didn't know she was a midwife," Abigail said.

"Why would you?" her mother replied.

"Claire is a lot of things," Paul's mother added, but she didn't say anything more.

(

So it happened that close to the end of the receiving line, when their smiles were worn out and their feet were sore and all the two of them could think about was sitting down, Abigail and Paul were faced with John and Claire Joseph.

Claire came first, shaking Paul's hand lightly. Her skin was dry, cool, and soft to the touch. It was impossible to tell, just by seeing her, how old she was: her skin was a golden colour, rich and wrinkled, pulled tight in some places, loose in others. Around her eyes were tracks like a bird might make, her smile etched there, ineffably. Her voice, when she spoke, was like the sound of dry leaves and the wind. "It was a lovely wedding," almost too quiet to hear.

"Thank you," Paul said, not sure of what else to say.

She covered their two hands, still joined, with her other hand, and said, quietly but plainly, "You love your wife." It was not an observation—it was a command, undeniable in its understated power.

"Yes ma'am," he said, lowering his eyes to the floor, unable to meet her golden gaze.

"Good." She moved along past him to where Abigail was standing. Before taking her hand, though, she took a step back and just looked at her. Paul watched her seeing, knowing how beautiful his wife looked, but seeing her again through another's eyes and finding it confirmed, over and over.

And then, instead of taking her hand, Claire leaned over and, stretching on her tiptoes, kissed Abigail on her smooth cheek, saying, "I'll be seeing you."

Abigail said later that she smelled of wild apples.

Paul was barely even aware of shaking John's hand, and the old man didn't say a word to him. And soon the receiving line was done, and they sat down at the table for the toasts and dinner and dancing, and John and Claire Joseph were the furthest thing from their minds.

❦

That was the wedding. Afterward, they went back to the house that had been the gift of both their parents and began their lives together. They both worked—Paul was apprenticed to a carpenter on the edge of the town, while Abigail worked at the feed supply. When not working, though, they spent all the time they could together, just the two of them, building their lives in the new little house. And it wasn't long, early summer, before Abigail realized that they were going to have a baby.

She didn't keep it a secret from Paul—she told him as soon as she knew herself. They were both so happy: it felt as if everything were coming together.

And the next weekend, when they were both free, they went to the house of John and Claire Joseph.

Neither of them drove, so they walked to John and Claire's house. It wasn't very far, and the distance passed quickly, laughing and jumping, cutting through fields, over fences, hopping over rows of corn that, only knee high, would soon be taller than they were.

They came out of the last field in the back yard. It was a tiny house, nestled snug on one side against a garden, lush and green already, with a chicken pen close to the back door and a small yard with a cat curled on the lawn in the sun. John Joseph was sitting on the back stoop, a mug next to him, looking out toward the field. He raised his hand in greeting as soon as they emerged, and called toward the garden, "Mother, they've arrived."

Claire's head appeared from where she'd been weeding the garden, a kerchief tied over her white hair. She stood up slowly as they walked toward her. She was wearing overalls, and her hands were full with weeds. They stopped at the edge of the garden and she came out to meet them.

"I've been expecting you," she said, by way of a greeting, dropping the weeds on a pile at the edge of the lawn.

Paul and Abigail looked at one another.

Claire shook her head and smiled broadly, revealing a mostly toothless mouth. "I was actually expecting you a little sooner. I could tell just by looking at you at your wedding that the two of you both had a little wildness in you. It's no wonder you couldn't wait 'til after you were married."

They both looked to the ground.

"Oh, stop your blushing, both of you," Claire exclaimed. "When you get to my age you've learned not to make any sort of judgements about other people's lives. It doesn't make any difference to me. I just like to see two people that are happy together. And you two look happy to me."

Paul and Abigail looked at one another, and blushed anyway.

"Are you happy about the baby that she's carrying?" she asked Paul, stepping closely enough to him that he could feel her breath and looking up into his face, so he couldn't look away. "Oh, don't act so surprised. Why else would the two of you have come out here? I make a good cup of coffee, but it isn't that good. What I want to know is if you think you can be a good father to this child."

Paul was very aware of both sets of eyes on him. "I think so."

Claire nodded. "I'm glad you didn't just say yes, assume you knew everything." She tapped the side of her head. "Shows you're not stupid."

Turning toward the house, Claire took Abigail by the arm and began walking. "We'll go in and I'll get out of my gardening clothes and into my mothering clothes and we'll take a look at you." Turning toward Paul, she added, "You I'll get a cup of coffee for, and you can keep John company trying to keep that stoop up. This is woman's business."

Paul didn't feel like he could argue.

❧

Paul sat on the stoop next to John Joseph, a steaming mug of coffee in his hand. The day had turned out hot, but there was a cool wind blowing out over the corn, seeming to come from the woods behind the field. He took a sip from his mug. "Your wife was right. This is a good cup of coffee."

John smiled, creasing his face in the same way as his wife's. "It's from the city. We get it in the mail." He straightened his legs out over the two steps, and Paul noticed for the first time that he was wearing grey wool socks without shoes. There was a hole near the toe on his left foot.

John set his mug down on the stoop. "Do you know Jacki Constantine? Ray and Mia's oldest girl?"

Paul shrugged. "Vaguely. I'd know her to see her."

"Well, she's a few years older than you, I suppose. Anyway, she's a college teacher in the city. She's the one who sends us the coffee. She's one of ours. She knows how much coffee we go through, so every two weeks or so we open up the mailbox and there's a parcel with a letter and a couple of pounds of coffee. Regular as clockwork." He took a sip from his own mug. "I've gotten pretty partial to it over the last few years."

"You folks have been delivering babies for a long time, I guess." Paul took another sip of his coffee.

John shook his head vigorously. "I don't deliver 'em. That's not my place. I'm out here, usually just like we're sittin' here now. But yeah, we've been at it for a while. Hell, we delivered your daddy, what, forty years ago? Forty-five?"

"That *is* a long time."

John smiled. "I guess it seems that way when you're twenty."

Paul craned his neck to look behind them, to the back door, almost willing it to open. But it stayed closed. "Is it always like this, the husbands sitting out on the back porch?"

"Where would you want to be?"

He gestured toward the house, but John shook his head. "Oh no, you don't want to be in there. That's a place for women, not men. I know, it's nothing you haven't seen before. Hell, as soon as you start living with someone and follow them into the bathroom you think you've got it all figured out, and that there aren't any more secrets possible between the two of you, but that's not so. And that," he gestured toward the closed door, "that's the biggest secret you can imagine. Even for me. All that Lamaze stuff, men in giving birth with their wives. And they call *that* natural."

Paul started to say something, but as if on cue, the door opened up and Abigail bounced across the stoop to him. "Paul," she said excitedly. "Claire says that everything looks really good. Really really good. Right?" She looked behind herself to where Claire was coming out of the house, dressed in a flower print dress.

Claire nodded. "You're gonna have a big healthy baby, about a month before your wedding anniversary. So you just take it easy, eat right, and come out to see us every so often." She looked directly at Paul. "Both of you. I don't want you feeling left out." She smiled at him as she sat down on the stoop on the opposite side of John. "And what'd you think of my coffee?"

{

He managed to be patient until that night when they were curled up in bed under a single sheet against the summer heat, the light from the partially open bathroom door spilling across the foot of the bed. Abigail was, at age twenty, still reluctant to sleep in the dark, and it made Paul happy to leave a light on for her.

"So, what did the two of you do in there?" he asked, not even sure he should be asking.

"In where?" she asked from where she lay nestled on his arm.

"When you and Claire Joseph were in the house for so long."

"Oh." She lifted herself on her elbow to look at him in the dim light. "We drank tea."

"What? I thought this was going to be some sort of consultation."

"Well, it was." She lay back down and stared up at the ceiling. "She told me just what she told you—that the baby was going to be due in about mid-March, and that it would be big and healthy."

It was Paul's turn to lift himself up. "But how did she know that? Did she do any tests or anything?"

"She just knew. She touched my stomach and she just knew." Unconsciously, her hand drifted to her belly, and began to rub it in a slow circle.

"That's it? She just touched you?" Paul sat upright, the sheet falling off him.

"Yeah, that's all."

"And that's okay with you? You don't need anything else, any *real* information? Like from a doctor?"

She shook her head. "You don't understand. I felt so safe, so secure when I was in there with her. I think she knows what she's doing. She *has* done it a time or two before."

Paul lay back down, and she curled against him. "Still, we should make an appointment with the doctor for you tomorrow, okay? I'll feel better if you see someone who knows what's going on."

"Will it make you fall asleep?"

He just smiled and pulled her closer to him, kissing her on the forehead.

But he lay there and listened to her as she fell asleep, the steady sway of her breathing, and for a long time after, just stared at the ceiling.

They didn't even need an appointment: Doctor Evans saw them almost as soon as they walked into the office. He opened the swinging door for Abigail, and led them through his office and into the examining room in back. Both of them had been in the room countless times, but Paul still felt a flutter as he first looked at the black vinyl table.

Abigail hopped onto the table without being prompted.

"What I would like you to do, Paul," Doctor Evans said, running his fingers along his thin white hair to smooth it down, "is to come and keep me company in the office while Abby puts on this gown, then I'll come in and see what I can find out for you, and we'll both let you know what's what. Okay?"

Paul shook his head. "Actually, I'd like to stay in here while you do the examination and everything, if that's all right with you."

It was the doctor's turn to shake his head. "I'm sorry, but that's . . . I just don't think that would really work out." He put his hand on Paul's shoulder, and with a gentle pressure began to guide him toward the book-lined office. "There's coffee in the pot, or cold drinks in the little bar fridge. We'll be out in just a few minutes, okay?"

The connecting door sliding shut behind them cut off any response.

Doctor Evans returned from the examining room no more than ten minutes later, but it felt like a week to Paul. He caught a glimpse of Abigail in the starched white gown through the door before the doctor slid it shut.

He played with his stethoscope as he spoke. "Well, Abby is quite healthy, and very pregnant. Congratulations."

Paul nodded.

"But I understand that you already knew that."

Paul cleared his throat. "We were out to see Claire Joseph yesterday." He felt almost embarrassed telling the doctor. "She said that Abigail was due in about mid-March."

"March seventeenth, actually, give or take a few days." He wandered through the office, and sat down behind his desk. "Paul, I want to tell you something. The Josephs are good people. They do good work. Now, I've treated both you and Abby your whole lives, and I certainly have no objection to bringing your child into the world, but, to be honest with you, you may be better off with Claire Joseph. I know that's not what you were expecting to hear, but that's the whole of it. When my wife was pregnant, both times, we went to Claire and John. Now, it's up to you. As I say, I'm more than willing. . . ."

Paul felt two warm hands on his shoulders, and he looked up to see Abigail, fully dressed, standing behind him. "We'll let you know," she said to the doctor, smiling.

He nodded back at her as Paul stood up. "Good. You do that."

{

"I can't believe it!" Paul said, as soon as they had closed the doctor's front door behind themselves. "Is he some sort of crackpot, or something? Maybe we should take the bus to Chilliwack and see if we can find a real doctor there."

"Paul," she said, taking his hand. "He *is* a real doctor."

"Then I don't get it. Why is he recommending we go to a midwife, instead of just saying he'll deliver the baby? What sort of a doctor is that?"

"He's a good doctor. *That's* why he's suggesting we should go back to see Claire. He knows what's best for me, and what's best for the baby. And I think he's right. I felt more comfortable with

Claire than I did in that examining room today."

"Yeah, but nobody likes doctors. You're supposed to feel uncomfortable when you go there."

She shook her head. "No, it's not that. It felt right to be at Claire's. It felt like she knew more than any doctor would. I don't know why, but I just know that it's the right thing for me. It's what I *need*."

They walked the rest of the way home in silence.

So the months passed in that way. The baby within Abigail grew, from the size of a peanut to the size of a tightly clenched fist, and gradually, to the size of an open hand. And Abigail grew too, at first, barely noticeably, but then, almost overnight, she widened and swelled, the baby setting low-down, her body rounding and glowing. And Paul, who thought on their wedding night that she was the most beautiful girl he had ever seen, fell in love with her all over again, correcting himself every time he looked at her: no, *this* is the most beautiful I have ever seen her. . . . At night, where they had used to sleep facing one another, their faces and breaths virtually one, they began to sleep spoon fashion, his body fitting around hers, one arm under her head, one arm wrapped around her belly or over her breasts, as if something could happen to her while she was sleeping, and he wouldn't allow it. The winter months were a time of growing.

They became regular visitors at the farm, Paul sitting on the front stoop with John while Abigail disappeared inside with Claire, emerging a while later with a progress report. Occasionally, Paul would get up the nerve to ask John, "So what are they doing in there?"

John would only shrug, and take a swallow of his coffee. "I have absolutely no idea."

And Paul would look out over the fallow fields, not knowing what to think.

Paul and Abigail walked to the farm every time, always trying out new routes, trying to find the shortest path between the two houses, for use when her time came. Claire told Abigail what to expect, what to look for to indicate that labour was coming on. And late one afternoon in March, it began.

"Paul!" He heard her calling him from the kitchen in his workshop in the basement. He knew, just from the sound of her voice, what was going on. He dropped the plane onto the board that would form one side of the cradle—an early anniversary gift—and vaulted up the stairs, taking them two at a time.

She was already in her jacket by the time he reached her. Her face was bright red, covered in a light sheen of sweat. "Are you okay?" he asked, pulling on his jacket.

She nodded.

"Should I call my father and have him give us a ride over, or are you okay to walk?" He pulled on his shoes without tying them.

"No, I'm fine. I'll be fine with walking over." She took a cup off the table and placed it gently in the sink.

"Are you sure? Because he said to call. Are you okay? Does it hurt?"

"Paul, relax. It doesn't hurt. I'll be fine until we get there. Plenty of time. Plenty of time."

He grabbed the packed bag from under the table. "Are you sure, because you look all flushed. Are you hurting?"

"No, I'm *excited*. Paul, we're having a baby."

And that stopped him cold in his tracks, suddenly realizing, fully completely, for the first time, the enormity of what was going on.

"Do you want to go to the hospital? Because we can call Doctor Evans and have him meet us there."

"Paul, let's just do it this way. This is what we've been preparing for."

"Okay," he said, suddenly sobered. "Let's get going."

"Not until you tie your shoes."

They left through the back door.

John was sitting in his usual place as they came through the field, not yet planted. He'd been able to see them coming for over a quarter mile through the fields in the dusk, and as they stepped into the yard, he called out, "They're here, mother."

Claire appeared at the door as Paul was helping Abigail up the steps to the porch. "It's started?"

Abigail just nodded, climbing the first step, and Claire nodded back. "Well, come inside girl. We'll get you ready to have a baby." She turned to her husband. "Are you ready?"

"Just let me get my jacket. It's gonna be a little cold tonight." He stood up and disappeared into the house.

"And Abigail, you come over here and kiss this sad lookin' young man goodbye. You'll be a different woman when you come back."

Abigail leaned over and they embraced, the baby solid between them, kissing quickly, fleetingly, before she turned away.

"Now you get into the house, girl, get out of the cold," Claire said, following Abigail through the doorway. She met John as he was coming out. "Take good care of this boy," she said, loudly enough for Paul to hear. "He looks scared enough to bolt."

"You take care of your business and I'll take care of mine," he said, zipping up his coat. "Now get inside." He smiled and they kissed quickly before she disappeared, closing the door behind herself.

John sat down on the stoop in his usual spot and lifted his mug. "I'd offer you a cup," he said, "but we've got things we have to be doing."

Paul pulled his arms tightly around himself, shivering even though he was sweating inside his down jacket. "What sort of things?"

"Just let me finish my coffee. Just because you don't have one is no reason to let mine go to waste." He drained the mug with one swallow and set it back down on the stoop. Rising slowly, he said, "Okay, let's you and me go for a little walk."

They set off through the barren fields, the woods looming dark ahead of them as the sun sank toward the horizon.

(

Abigail was wearing only a white shift, lying on her back in John and Claire's bed. Claire was clearing the top of the dresser, laying out bowl, fresh towels, and a small tray of stainless steel instruments. From the kitchen came a whistling sound. "That'd be my water boiled."

Abigail laughed. "You mean you really boil water for delivery?"

Claire snorted. "No, of course not. You boil water for tea to have while you're waiting. Would you like a cup?"

Abigail shook her head.

""All right," Claire said. "I'll be right back."

Abigail's contraction started the moment Claire disappeared through the doorway. It took her breath away and she couldn't even scream. Though she wanted to.

(

The woods were dim, but there was enough light from the rising moon to see the trail before them and to avoid tripping over branches or stones in their path.

They walked in silence, until Paul asked, "What are we doing out here? Shouldn't we be back at the house in case they need any help?"

John shook his head. "I told you before. That's not our place. There's nothing that can happen that our help is going to do anything but make worse. And that's a fact."

"So what're we going to do? Just walk around out here until it's all over? Hunt wild cigars?"

John snickered. "No. We've got our things to do. Be on the lookout for dry wood. We'll be needing to build a fire."

(

"One hit while I was away, didn't it?" Claire asked, coming back into the bedroom with a steaming cup of tea.

Abigail just nodded, her face wet with a sheen of new sweat.

Claire set her tea down on the dresser and, picking up a damp cloth, sponged off Abigail's face. "I always say that the first contractions are the worst, because they take you so much by surprise, and nothing anybody says or describes to you can even hint at what it's really going to be like when it happens."

"Does that mean this is the worst it'll get?" Abigail gasped, feeling oddly like she had just run for several hours,

Claire laughed. "Oh no, it'll get much, much worse. It just won't take you quite as surprise."

"God, there has to be a better way than this to have children."

Claire shook her head. "Oh, no. There's no better way than this."

{

It seemed to Paul that they had been walking for hours, picking up chunks of windfall branches, before they finally came to a tiny clearing and John dropped his armload on the ground.

Paul followed suit, then took a look around.

It was already difficult to see: the sun had long since sunk below the horizon, and the light was fading quickly. But Paul could see enough. The clearing wasn't large, but bounded by almost impenetrable dark walls of forest on all sides. It was crossed through the middle by a small creek, playing quietly along its stony bed, its banks lined with a fine sand that shimmered white.

John took several of the branches and walked to the edge of the creek where he began building a fire on a blackened site that looked like it had seen many fires before.

"What is this place?" Paul asked. "I've been all over these woods since I was a boy and I've never even seen this place."

"This is not a place for boys," John said, without looking up.

{

Claire left Abigail by herself in the bedroom, and went quietly out the back door. Climbing down from the stoop, she went to the garden.

In the centre of the garden, where the carrots would be later in the spring, was a wide, shallow basin, filled with rain water. Crouching, Claire picked it up and carried it over to the lawn where she set it down again. She knelt next to it.

Softly, almost imperceptibly, she began to sing. At the same time she sang, she traced her fingertips over the surface of the water drawing liquid symbols that matched the words that she sang.

The secret, she knew, was not to pull down the moon. Rather, it was easier to catch it before it was fully risen in the first place. Easier for a woman of her age.

As she sang and traced her symbols into the water, the moon rose there, shimmering in the basin, its surface bent and refracted by the symbols she traced over it. And the sky remained dark and moonless.

For the moon in the basin was the real, true moon, full and heavy, round almost to the point of bursting.

And as she finished singing, as her fingers trailed off and dried themselves on her dress, Claire whispered, to the moon in the basin of rainwater, "Wait."

John had gotten the fire going, and the flames licked against the dark sky. They both sat on smooth stones at the edge of the creek, the fire between them, just at the line between the stones and the white sand, which glowed orange in the firelight.

"What *is* this place?" Paul asked again.

And this time, John Joseph answered him. "In a sense, this place is a metaphor. There," he gestured behind them, at the dark forest from which they had come, "is forest, but here is just creek and stones. Sort of a boundary place between two worlds. And that," he pointed at where the creek came from the forest. "Is the source of it all. Its birthplace. I don't know what happens before, out in the trees. There's run-off, and groundwater, and swampy patches, but here, I do know." He dipped his hand in the cold, rushing water. "We have a creek. Like it had always existed, but only came into its own here."

"We came all the way out here for a metaphor?" Paul asked incredulously.

"That's part of it," John said. "But there is magic in metaphor."

And Paul realized suddenly what had been bothering him for some time. "Isn't it supposed to be the full moon tonight? Where is the moon?"

"That," John said, "is part of it also."

{

When Claire returned to the bedroom, Abigail had suffered through another contraction, and didn't say anything to her as Claire took a sip of her tea and sat down in the chair at the side of the bed.

"How are you doing?" she asked softly, brushing the sweaty hair back from Abigail's forehead.

She smiled weakly. "I don't think I'm too fond of this."

Claire smiled back. "Well, let's take a look at you," she said, pulling back the covers and lifting the hem of her shift. "Looks good. It'll be a while yet, though." She glanced out the window, into the darkness.

"What will we do?" Abigail asked, in a voice that sounded almost like a sob.

Claire laid her hand on the firm tautness of Abigail's belly, where it was cool against the heat, and whispered, as she had to the moon, "Wait."

{

John stood up. "The moon is women's magic, you see. It has no place in what we have to do here tonight." He crouched down across from Paul and unzipped his jacket. "For that, we need man's magic: earth, fire, and blood." It was then that Paul noticed for the first time the hunting knife on his belt.

"What are you talking about?"

John pulled the knife from its sheath, watching Paul's eyes on it in the firelight. "It's beautiful, isn't it?" he said softly.

Paul nodded. The handle of the knife seemed to glow with a creamy warmth, and the blade burned blue in the darkness.

"It was made for me," John continued. "The shank is ivory, with inlaid horn. The blade is . . ." He stopped suddenly, looking around the clearing as if he had heard something in the darkness.

"We should begin," he said simply, and spun the knife in his hand. Using its shank, he drew a circle in the sand between Paul's feet.

"Much though others will argue, birthing isn't about science or medicine or technology. It's about magic. Women's magic. Blood, water and the moon. It's not a medical process—it's about creating life from within. Do you understand that?"

Paul nodded.

"And there's no holding that back, no matter what. Abby's going to have your baby tonight, no matter what happens out here." John took off his jacket and laid it on the sand behind him. "But there are things that *should* be done before that happens. Natural things. Things that have been forgotten or overlooked. Becoming a mother is part biological, and part magical. And it's that magical part, whether you know it or not, that makes a good mother."

He stood up for a moment and stretched upwards, then crouched in front of Paul.

"Take off your coat."

Paul did as he was told, the side of him closest to the fire still warm, his other side cold.

"But that's only half of it. Every child has two parents. That's two kinds of magic, but the man's magic is usually ignored, or forgotten. Men don't have babies. They've got the biological part down pat, but they don't have any experience of the magic. When you think about having your child, are you afraid?"

He nodded.

"Do you feel helpless? Like you don't know what's going on?"

He nodded again.

"Well, that has to change before you can hope to be any kind of a father at all. Being a father is more than biology. It's earth and fire and blood."

John reached out, took Paul's left wrist in his right hand, and gently extended Paul's arm. "The next time you see your father, ask to see his arms. Look very carefully. This is man's magic." He extended the knife in his left hand toward Paul's left arm. "Tell me your fears about your child. As many as you can think of."

There was something spellbinding about the fire, the sound of the breeze in the darkening trees, the cool smoothness of John's voice. Paul felt his fears well up inside him, everything he had tried to push down for the past nine months, everything he had denied while he was being strong and supportive, everything he had thought he had resolved, all coming back from within him in a rush. The words spilled out, with such a force that he didn't even notice the razor edge of John's knife cutting thin lines into his arm, matching a single cut for each fear.

"I'm afraid he'll be born dead"

cut

"or handicapped"

cut

"or not born at all"

cut

"I'm worried that . . ."

As he cut, John sang softly under his breath, the words holding the knife steady as he gently rocked, guiding the blade into the lattice work it was creating, locating the skin when there was too much blood to see. He didn't even hear the list of fears, concentrating instead on the cuts, each opening like a tiny puckered mouth, thin and perfect, the blood flowing freely, pooling in the circle in the sand at Paul's feet. With the last fear, the blade stopped moving, of its own accord.

Paul didn't even look at his arm, or the blood that welled onto the ground. Instead, his gaze was locked on John's face, his golden eyes, his barely moving lips. The air hummed with the fading echoes of his chant. John gently released his arm, and, switching the knife to his right hand, gently grasped Paul's right wrist with his left hand.

"Now," he said, his voice sounding as if it was coming from another place altogether, "Tell me your hopes for your child."

And the process began again, Paul's head filling with hopes, dreams, ambitions, his own and those he had already wished on his son. The words spilled from him, as the blood spilled from his right arm, from the intricate tracing of cuts, spilling to the ground and mixing with the blood already there. And John sang again, the same song, different words guiding the knife, halting it as the litany concluded.

Without saying a word, he stood up, laying the knife on the ground where he had been kneeling, and walked to the fire. Without hesitation, he reached into the light, past the flames, into the coals, taking a handful that felt almost cool to the touch, but which seared and smoked as he held them and walked to the water. Plunging his hand under the surface, the coals hissed and burst, cooling almost instantly.

He crushed the coals in his hand and dropped the stiff, black mud into the bloody circle at Paul's feet.

Paul looked at him.

"This," he said, "is man's magic. Blood, fire, and earth. Now, shape." He gestured to the circle.

And Paul knew, without being told, what to do, as if it had been within him the entire time. As if he had always known.

He plunged his hands into the circle of sand at his feet, warm with his blood and the embers, and began to shape. And from the mud, the coals, and his own blood, there emerged a form, a perfect, tiny child, dark, dun-coloured and still. His hands moved of their own accord, until they held between them, perfect in every way, his child. He held it up, toward John, toward the sky.

And John spoke. "That is your child, made of the earth, the ash, and the blood of your hopes and fears for it. It has no life, for a child made up of the hopes and fears of its parents is no child: it may live, but it cannot survive, cannot ever prosper, cannot ever be its own life. In order for this child to live, it must come into the world of its own hopes, its own fears. Yours must be washed away." As he spoke, the child grew heavier in Paul's hands, and he felt a throbbing move through him, from the ground at his feet and up toward the child, which slowly turned its head toward its father, and opened its eyes. They were dun-coloured, flat, reflecting only the orange glow of the fire, nothing of any inner light.

Without being told, simply knowing, Paul walked to the water. Kneeling there, holding between his hands the child that he had created, the child that looked silently up to him with one eye of brown and one eye of green, he lowered it to the water, and watched, tears rolling down his cheeks, as the water rushed across the small form, washing away the blood of his hopes and fears, the ash and the sand, until his hands were clean, and empty. As he stood up, John was behind him, and held him as he cried.

"It is done," he said to the sky.

In the backyard, near the garden, as if she had heard, Claire dipped her hands into the basin, and taking a double handful of water, flung the moon, fully formed, back into the sky.

From the house, a hoarse scream echoed through the silvery night, and a shower of cold rainwater fell on Claire Joseph. She ran her wet hands through her damp hair, and turned back into the house.

Her hands were still cold and wet as she laid them, side by side, on Abigail's stretched belly, and she began to sing. "Breathe," she said, interrupting her song.

Abigail's face was covered in sweat, her hair sticking to her forehead, and standing in clumps where she had pulled it. Blood ran down her chin from where she had bitten through her lip.

"When will this be over?" She choked, her voice thick with phlegm and rough from screaming. "I just want this to be over."

"Shhhh," sighed Claire Joseph, reaching for her hand. She swayed at the side of the bed, as if dancing to an unheard music. "Not long now."

Another contraction, and she sang louder, dipping her hands

under the hem of Abigail's gown, where the sheet was warm and wet, then laying her palms on her belly, where she was still glazed with the moonlit rainwater. "Blood, water, and the moon," she said quietly, as Abigail screamed one last time, her voice mingling with that of her child, screaming out its first breath in the cold world.

"John," she called, her voice catching in her throat. "You can both come in here, now."

And from the back stoop came the sound of footfalls, and both men appeared in the room as if by magic. Paul's face was drawn and wan and white as the moonlight through the window, his arms and hands brown with dried blood, but Claire knew he wouldn't be feeling that, any more than John was feeling the burns on his hands.

As soon as he came through the door, as soon as he saw Abigail on the bed, he was at her side, crouched next to her. "Are you okay?" he asked, urgently.

She nodded, unable to keep herself from crying. "Yeah. Where were you?" The question was almost frantic.

"I was out walking. With John." He glanced behind himself at the older man in the doorway. "I'll tell you about it sometime."

"I had a baby," she said, as if she couldn't quite believe it herself.

And for the first time, looking away from her face, he saw their child laying at her breast, eyes open, brown and rimed with white and wet, looking up at their faces.

"Well, you can go pick it up," Claire said, not quite brusquely. "It's not gonna bite you."

He stood up, and lifted the child with an exaggerated care that John and Claire knew would take another birth to ween him from.

And as he stood there, looking at his child, he realized that it was nothing at all like he had hoped for, and nothing at all like he had feared, and he felt Abigail's sweat damp hand against his arm as his daughter looked up at him for the first time.

THE CRYING IN THE WALLS

The key hesitated in the lock, and Curt had to jiggle it slightly to get it to turn. When the tumblers released, it was with a soft pop like the cork on a bottle of wine sliding free, as if a seal had been broken.

He also remembered to lift the doorknob slightly as he turned it, and to push the door more firmly than one might expect to get it to open.

"Well, you have to understand, it's an old house," he said, smiling, as the door swung open into the empty vestibule.

The phrase had become a running joke between them over the past several weeks. They had heard it so often from the realtors, from their mortgage broker, from the lawyer who had drawn up the transfer, that they could recite it verbatim, significant pauses intact.

"But it's ours," Laura said, a half-step behind him as she finished her part of the patter.

His smile broadened and he stepped into their new house, almost a century old. The air seemed to echo, sharp with plaster and hardwood, the smell of floor polish and lingering traces of cinnamon and apple. The realtor had had a pie baking during their third walk-through, the semi-detached house warm and inviting with the smell. As if they needed to be convinced. As if they hadn't known the first time they walked through that tricky front door, caught their first glimpse of the shining floors, the colossal staircase that stretched to the second floor landing above the fourteen-foot ceiling. Laura had squeezed Curt's hand as the agent detailed the selling points, her grip tightening and tightening as she tried to maintain her poker face.

"Honey, we're home!" Curt said broadly, for effect, turning to see if she was smiling, if she was allowing herself to savour the moment.

She was still standing on the porch, the toes of her sandals snug up to the line of the doorway.

She was looking at him, half-smiling.

She waited a beat.

Then another.

Then, finally, "Aren't you supposed to carry me over the threshold?"

He almost laughed; she looked so earnest, but with that gleam in her eye. "I think that's after you get married," he said, stepping toward her. "Not when you buy a house. Especially—" he let the word hang as he looked meaningfully down at the solid roundness of her belly "—when you're—"

"Don't you dare."

"—as big as a house."

"Asshole," she said. "What was that the doctor said about not upsetting the pregnant woman?"

But she was smiling, and he trailed his fingers over her belly as he reached to take her hand.

"Welcome home," he said quietly as he led her inside.

She trailed her fingers along the rough plaster under the empty coat-hooks as she followed.

They didn't unpack most of the boxes—plates enough for Indian take-out, a glass for Curt's wine, a mug for Laura's tea—but Curt made sure to find the carton marked "Bedroom—Bedding."

He made up the bed, even though the mattress and box spring were floating in the centre of the room, the frame in pieces against one wall.

"We could have just slept on the air mattress," Laura protested when she came into the bedroom, breathing heavily from climbing the stairs.

"Don't be silly," he said, gesturing at the bed, as if putting on sheets and pillowcases and a duvet were an achievement. "You're not sleeping on an air mattress."

She had taken, almost as soon as she learned she was pregnant, to resting her hand on the swell of her abdomen. She rubbed it in a small circle as he drew back the covers for her.

It was hours later, in the dark of their new house, surrounded by new creaks and groans, that she heard it.

She started awake. Curt was holding her from behind, his arm curled over her bump.

Her eyes wide, she tried to make sense of where she was. Sharp angles, shadowy blocks, it took her a moment to remember that she was in their bed, a soft island in a sea of boxes and confusion.

But what was that sound?

It seemed to be coming from that corner. No, just to the left. The right, maybe?

What was that?

She tensed, starting to turn to sit up, but Curt snuggled in, his arm close around her, his face nuzzled into the back of her neck.

It was almost impossible to hear anything over the sound of his breath in her ear. But something had woken her.

Something . . .

She willed herself to listen more closely, to tune out the gentle half-rasp of Curt asleep.

She strained.

Nothing.

She hadn't realized how quickly her heart had been beating until it started to slow.

That can't be good for the baby.

As her pulse calmed, her whole body relaxed, seeming to sink back into the mattress.

Her eyelids grew heavy.

Her breath thickened.

She thought of the baby. And something about a circus. Ringmaster. Acrobats. About witnessing pink elephants. Thoughts she knew, even as she was having them, were the nonsense of almost-asleep.

And just as she had that realization, as she was about to slip away into sleep, she heard it again.

This time she sat up, Curt's arm dropping away from her as she pushed herself upward. He flopped onto his back and began to snore.

"Jesus Christ," she muttered, straining to hear again.

Yes, there it was. Near the corner.

She dropped her left hand to her belly.

It was a faint sound, not quite distinct, distant, a faint mewling, like a kitten in the next room.

No.

She listened more closely as she stood up, as she carefully crossed the room in the half-light.

Not a kitten.

Closer to the wall, she could hear it more clearly.

It was a baby.

There was no mistaking it, the sound, that high, thick desperate sound, or the effect, the ache she felt in her breasts, her belly.

She could feel the cry. Was the baby hungry? Frightened? Alone? Her sister would know; she would know soon enough.

The crying was coming from a spot not far from the corner of the room, along the wall that would be to the left side of the bed once the bedroom was set up.

The wall that they shared with the neighbours.

The neighbours.

Of course. A new baby.

That made sense.

A moment later, the crying stopped.

She smiled as she padded back to bed, slipping between the warm flannel sheets, imagining another bedroom just on the other side of the wall, a mother going into the dark, the light of a hallway falling across the crib as she picked up the crying baby.

Or a father. It could be the father.

Curt had curled onto his other side on the far edge of the bed, his back like the shell of some insect or sea creature, curved and hard and resistant. He didn't stir as she adjusted herself in the bed, as she struggled to get comfortable.

No, probably not the father.

Laura fell back to sleep with her left hand on her belly, listening to Curt breathe, imagining their new neighbours.

❧

He made breakfast—oatmeal and a half grapefruit each—while she was still asleep. He was about to go up and wake her when he heard the sound of her heavy steps on the staircase.

He flipped the switch on the kettle to re-boil the water.

"Good morning," he said as she came into the kitchen.

He moved in for a quick kiss, but she turned sleepily away.

"I made you some breakfast," he said, unfazed. "And the tea—" the kettle clicked off "—will be right up."

She sat down at the table. Her hair was dishevelled; she was still half-asleep. "The top stair is loose," she said, her first words of the day.

He sat the tea in front of her, next to the grapefruit. "What?"

"The top stair," she said, curling her hands around the mug. "The board wiggles."

"I'll take care of it," he said, sitting down across from her. "Sorry. I couldn't find the brown sugar." He tilted his hands helplessly.

"This is okay," she said.

He watched her staring into the bowl as if transfixed. It took her a long moment to come back to herself. "Thank you," she said, glancing over at him. "For making breakfast."

He held his tie back and leaned over his bowl to eat, watching her the whole time. She picked at her oatmeal, stirring it, lifting spoonfuls only to dump them back into the bowl. She did eat a couple of bites, though. Better than nothing. Better than some days.

"I know you're going to want to get at the unpacking," he said, looking down at his bowl. "But it's Friday, and it's a short day for me. You should just take it easy today, and we can spend the weekend making this place homey."

"I can start on it," she said. "I'm not an invalid."

He reached his hand across the table.

She ignored it.

"I know you're not an invalid. I just don't want you to—"

"Drive myself crazy?"

"—stress yourself out," he finished over her.

Their eyes met, and locked.

"I know you're not an invalid," he repeated, his voice low and warm. "I just want you to be careful."

Her smile was tight and pinched. "I'll be careful." She leaned back in her chair, resting her hands on her belly. "I think that's enough breakfast."

He looked at the churned, solidified bowl of oatmeal, the untouched grapefruit, at her hands.

{

She wanted to start in the bedroom, to get rid of those stacks of boxes, to see the closet full of their clothes, to see the top of the bureau cluttered with jewellery and knickknacks and photographs again.

But the bureau was in pieces in the corner, near the bedframe, and she knew how Curt would react if he came home from work and found it built.

Better to let him have his moments of manliness where he could get them.

The kitchen, maybe.

Speaking of manliness. . . . The top step wasn't dangerous or anything, but it gave her a start when it seemed to tilt just slightly when she stepped on it.

Curt would take care of that, too.

It made her smile, the thought of him with his toolbox, filled with screwdrivers only used to change remote control batteries, the hammer that had only ever driven nails to hang pictures.

It was very sweet.

He was very sweet.

Patient. Kind.

He deserved better.

She would be better.

Curt had already partially unpacked several boxes, likely looking for the makings of breakfast. There was a cloth hung over the faucet, a tea towel on top of the stove.

She pulled a chair over to the counter and ran hot water onto the cloth. Steadying herself with one hand on the countertop, she climbed onto the chair and opened the cupboard door.

The previous owners had cleaned everything thoroughly before they left, but she scrubbed the insides of the cupboards with the dishcloth anyway, making sure to get into every corner, not forgetting to wash the undersides of each shelf.

She was careful each time she stepped down from the cupboard to rinse the cloth, each time she climbed back up.

She had originally planned to do all the cupboards, but by the time she was finished with the upper set she was sweating and breathing heavily. She pulled the chair back to the table and collapsed into it.

She would just rest for a minute, then she'd start unpacking some of the boxes. She'd leave the lower cupboards for Curt to clean. She probably shouldn't be—

The baby cried behind the wall.

Laura jumped.

It sounded like the baby was right there in the room with her, its cry deep and plangent.

Hungry, she thought.

As if in response, the baby cried louder, building to a level of breathlessness that made her heart ache.

Why wasn't someone picking it up? Why would you just let a baby cry like that?

She didn't know where the idea came from—it was completely unlike her—but once she had it, she couldn't shake it. She would go next door. She'd introduce herself. She'd offer to help.

She looked down at herself: she'd need to get dressed first.

As she went upstairs and looked for something to put on, she thought of what Dr. Talbot would say about her now. Confronting her fears. Getting out of herself. Meeting new people.

He'd probably be so proud.

By the time she got dressed, though, and made it back

downstairs, the crying had stopped.

She stood in the kitchen quiet, motionless, holding her breath and listening. Nothing. No crying, no faint, comforting voices.

She wouldn't bother them next door. She'd leave it, for the time being.

{

The crying woke her just before three A.M. that night.

Curt had put the bedframe together after he got home from work, and the bed was now in place, head to the north wall.

The crying seemed to be coming from where it had come from the night before, a spot on the east wall, a few feet to her left.

It was louder tonight. But then, she was closer.

But it wasn't just that.

The crying was louder.

The baby seemed . . . hungrier. More desperate. Crying itself into a small frenzy.

How could anyone sleep through that?

Curt snored behind her, and Laura dug her fingers into the bed under her pillow, willing the sound to stop.

God, won't someone pick that baby up?

Please, please, please . . .

{

"I can't believe you slept through that last night," were the first words out of Laura's mouth when she got downstairs the next morning.

Curt had been sitting at the table drinking coffee and reading the Saturday *Globe*, but he had jumped up when he heard her on the stairs and started making tea.

"Slept through what?" he asked, turning to face her.

"The baby."

He glanced down at her belly, then back up to her face. "What?"

"The baby last night," she said, as if that explained everything.

"Did something—" He took a step forward.

"Not *our* baby," she said, stepping back. "The baby next door."

"Next door?"

"It cries. I've heard it a few times. I'm surprised you could sleep through it."

"I didn't hear anything," he said, shaking his head. His brow was furrowed in thought, his face serious.

"Oh, I know *that*," she said. "You snored through the whole thing. I'm a little concerned."

He tilted his head.

"There's no way you're going to be allowed to sleep through the night once this one starts crying," she said, in a tone of stern admonishment that was only half-kidding, curving her hands around her belly.

"Yeah, okay," he said, brow still furrowed.

"Hey," she said, breaking into a smile. "Come back to me, space ranger."

"What?" He shook his head, shook it off.

"I was just kidding," she said. "No big deal."

"Yeah." His voice was still thoughtful, still far away.

"I'll wake you up next time," she said. "It'll be good practice."

{

She was awake that night when the baby started to cry. She had tried to sleep, but it wouldn't come, and as Curt slipped away, his breathing growing slow and regular, she gave up.

There is nothing lonelier than lying awake while the person you love slumbers next to you.

As the numbers slid soundlessly past on the clock radio, first twelve, then one, then two, she began to think that it wasn't going to happen, that maybe the baby would sleep through the night.

But at 2:42 A.M., the crying started again.

At first, it was a faint mewling, a shallow snuffling sound, like maybe the baby was just stirring in its sleep. After a moment, the first cry, a wail that cut through the wall, that made Laura ache, that made her belly clench.

She lay in bed, listening. Despite their conversation that

morning, she wasn't sure that she wanted to wake Curt; he was so cranky when he was disturbed.

But if it went on for too long—

"Shh."

She sat upright at the sound of the voice. It was so clear, so loud, it sounded like it was coming from just past the foot of the bed.

"Shh."

Without even being aware that she was doing it, she was standing up, walking toward the wall.

"It's okay. Shh. It's okay."

It was a child's voice.

Was it a boy or a girl?

Six, maybe seven years old, it didn't matter. It was a child. An older sibling, maybe. Comforting the baby.

As she touched her hand to the cold wall, the child started to sing.

"*Frère Jacques, frère Jacques. . . .*"

The words seemed to echo through the bedroom.

"Curt!" she shouted, turning back toward the bed. "Curt!"

She crossed the room in three steps as the song resonated around her, kneeling onto the bed, pushing Curt between his shoulder blades. "Curt, wake up!"

He groaned and turned partway over.

"*Dormez-vous, dormez-vous. . . .*"

"Curt, wake up!" She pushed on his shoulders, then hit him desperately. "Curt!"

He seemed to jump off the bed, his eyes flashing open. "What? What is it? Laura?" His voice was thick and slow, and he shook his head several times, trying to clear it. "Are you okay?"

"Listen," she said. "It's the baby."

"Something's wrong with the baby?"

She wanted to shake him. Instead, she grabbed his shoulders. "Curt, listen."

The room was as silent as an empty church.

They listened together for a long moment before Curt spoke. "Listen to what?"

She refused to give up, refused to breathe.

"Laura, are you okay?"

She nodded, afraid to speak.

"Laura?"

His voice seemed to be coming from very far away.

"I . . . I thought I heard something."

"The baby again?" he asked, all trace of sleep and confusion gone from his voice.

"Next door."

"Laura—"

"It's okay," she said, nodding firmly. "It's okay. I'm sorry I woke you up."

"Laura . . ."

"Go back to sleep," she said. "It's okay."

He lay back down and she snuggled in beside him, not touching him.

It took a long time for his breathing to slow again. She lay awake, listening. Waiting.

{

Curt wasn't alone when he got home from work.

"Dr. Talbot," she said, grateful that she had forced herself to get dressed. It had been almost too much to ask of herself, with not having slept the past couple of nights.

"Hello, Laura," he said gently, taking her hand. "How are you feeling?"

The doctor didn't miss the sharp glance she threw toward Curt.

"It's all right," Dr. Talbot said. "Curt asked if I would mind dropping by."

"Why don't you two go into the living room," Curt said. "I'll get a start on dinner."

"Thank you, Curt," the doctor said as Curt showed him into the living room, Laura following two steps behind.

"Yes, thank you Curt," she said, seething, as she sat down on the sofa.

"Don't be upset with Curt," Dr. Talbot said, allowing him a

moment to leave. "He's just worried about you."

"So you rushed over here at five-thirty on a Monday night?"

"He told me you hadn't been sleeping."

"Just a couple of nights."

"He's right to be worried."

"I'm all right," she said.

"You knew that there were risks with your pregnancy, given your—"

"Condition," she finished.

"And I told you that I'd be keeping a close eye on you."

"I'm all right," she repeated.

"You knew there were risks in going off your medication."

"I'm all right."

"Curt tells me you're hearing things."

"Oh, for fuck's sake."

"He's worried."

"I'm not *hearing things*." She stretched out the words derisively. "There's a baby next door—"

"Curt tells me it's keeping you awake at night."

"It's *crying*," she snapped. "God, what sort of a mother would I make if a crying baby didn't wake me up?"

"That's true."

"I'm fine, Dr. Talbot. Really. I'm sorry that Curt worried you."

"I'm just checking in."

"And I appreciate that."

He took a deep breath, exhaled slowly, through his mouth. "If things get bad, like they got last year—"

"They won't," she interrupted. "I'm fine. Really."

"—we won't be able to put you back on the regimen. Not until the baby is born. That's—"

"You don't have to worry."

"It's not just my job to worry, Laura," he said, almost in a whisper. "We've spent a lot of time together, you and I."

"I won't let you down."

"I'm not worried about you letting me down, Laura. I'm worried about you letting you down."

She tugged her sleeves down, twisting her sweatshirt cuffs in each fist. "I'm not going to hurt myself."

""You said that before," Curt said from the doorway. He was holding a tray with the teapot and two cups, a creamer and the sugar bowl.

Dr. Talbot looked at him, and shifted in the chair. "Curt, if you could just—"

"Right," he said, slipping the tray onto the table between them. "I'll get out of your hair."

The doctor started to say 'thank you,' but Laura was already standing up. "Actually, Dr. Talbot was just leaving."

Curt stopped.

Dr. Talbot stood up. "Laura, if you would just—"

"I'm all right, Dr. Talbot," she said. "I'm not hearing things, and I'm not going to hurt myself. I heard a baby crying. God, I'm a mother: what was I supposed to do, ignore it?"

She didn't wait for a response, brushing past Curt on her way to the stairs.

As she climbed toward the bedroom, she could hear Curt and the doctor's voices behind her, hushed. Curt apologizing, the doctor reassuring, asking him something about the neighbours.

She didn't care.

She made a point of slamming the bedroom door behind herself, sitting on the bed and staring at the wall.

{

"Are you all right?" Curt asked, coming into the bedroom. She had no idea how long it had been since the doctor had left, but it felt like quite a while. Perhaps he had been giving her some space, letting her cool down.

He had knocked before opening the door.

She hadn't answered.

He repeated the question.

"I'm fine," she said, not looking up at him, not coming close to meeting his eye.

"I'm sorry I called the doctor."

She barely heard the words. The baby had been crying for a

while, and he—Laura was sure it was a boy—was all she could focus on.

The deep, ragged breaths, the gasping, the wailing . . .

"Laura?"

"It's all right," she said blandly.

She knew better than to say anything else. Certainly knew better than to ask Curt if he could hear the baby.

She would sit on her hands. She wouldn't do anything, or say anything. Not yet. Not yet.

If it got too bad, she would call the doctor. It wasn't fair to Curt to let him go on like nothing was wrong. If he couldn't hear what was going on around him, it was up to her. She'd look after him. She'd take care of him.

That was her job.

That was the mommy's job, to take care of her boys.

The baby wailed, and she clenched her fists on the bedcovers, subtly, so Curt wouldn't see.

She didn't get out of bed.

Curt got up after the alarm clock rang for the second time, disappearing almost soundlessly through the bathroom door. A few moments later, the shower started.

She barely heard it.

Lying on her back, staring at the ceiling, all she could hear was the baby.

He was really wailing now, like he was starving. His brother was trying to soothe him, murmuring, "It's all right, it's all right, she'll come soon," but nothing helped. The baby kept screaming. Crying.

She tried covering her ears, pulling the pillow up around the sides of her face. She tried humming to herself, snatches of an old Wilco song that she couldn't quite remember. She tried holding her breath.

Curt came out of the bathroom just as she was about to start crying herself. She willed the tears back, forced herself to look cool and calm.

"It's all right. Shh."

"You're awake," Curt said from the bathroom doorway.

Laura nodded, not entirely trusting her voice.

"Did you sleep at all?"

"Shh, it's gonna be okay."

"A little bit," she lied as he crossed to the wardrobe and began pulling out clothes.

"She'll be here soon."

"Are you going to try for a bit more?"

It took her a moment to realize that Curt was still talking to her. The baby's cries had grown louder, closer: it was like he was right there. Like if she reached out of bed—

"Laura?"

"I think I'll get up." He was tying his tie. When had he gotten dressed? "Do you want breakfast?" She struggled herself up to a sitting position.

He shrugged into his jacket. "No, thanks. I've got an early meeting." He glanced at his watch. "And I . . ."

Tie. Watch. Jacket.

When had that happened?

"She's coming soon."

He was still talking, but she couldn't hear him. The baby and his brother were both right there, close enough to touch.

"Laura?"

She forced a smile. "You have a good day."

He stopped and stared at her. "Are you . . ."

The crying subsided to a faint, thick snuffling.

"I'm all right."

He didn't look convinced.

"I'll give you a call a little later," he said, leaning in to brush her hair back, to kiss her on the forehead. He seemed sad to be leaving.

"You don't have to," she said, swinging her legs off the bed. "I know you're busy."

His smile was pinched and tight. "I'll call," he said. "Okay?"

She nodded. He'd call. Of course he'd call. He was sweet. He was kind. He was worried.

He was going to be such a good dad.

The baby started crying again, the sound deeper, thicker, phlegmy.

"Okay."

"I love you," he said, as he turned away.

"I love you too."

She listened to his footsteps down the stairs, to the sound of the door closing behind him.

She was alone.

And the baby wailed.

¿

She wasn't sure how long she spent sitting on the edge of the bed, listening. It could have been a minute, it could have been an hour: time lost all meaning in the pain, the full-throated desperation of that cry.

When she finally stood up, it was to go to the bathroom. She peed, put on a pair of yoga pants from on top of the laundry hamper, and drew on her favourite hoodie before going downstairs, careful to hold the rail, especially at the very top.

Standing at the foot of the staircase, she savoured the silence for a moment. Nothing. No crying. No comforting murmurs. Just the distant hum of traffic, the shifting of a breeze.

She permitted herself a half-smile.

She set herself a spot at the head of the kitchen table, put some water on to boil, and was slicing an apple when the crying started again.

She jerked. Flinched. Turned.

It was like the baby was right in the kitchen, near the table. Under the table.

She actually crouched to look, bending with her back straight, her knees parted, craning her neck as if expecting to see a small boy hiding under the table like a fort, protecting his younger brother.

Protecting . . .

Was that it?

What were they doing next door to that poor baby? What had they done to that little boy that he needed to take care of an infant?

Without hesitating, she stormed out of the kitchen, wrenched the front door open, and stalked across the shared porch.

She pressed hard on the neighbour's doorbell, rolling on her feet.

She cursed herself inwardly for not having done this sooner. She should have called Child Services when she knew that something was wrong. Maybe this way was better, though. Give the parents a chance to change their ways, to let them know that whatever they were doing, it wasn't a secret, and if they—

"Hello?"

The voice was faint and frail, muffled by the door. There were curtains on the other side of the small window on the door, and Laura strained to see through, past her own reflection.

"Yes?"

"I'm—" Now that she was standing there, she had absolutely no idea what to say. "My name is Laura. My husband and I, we just moved in next door. . . ."

"Oh, the new neighbours." The door opened slowly, and Laura took a step back. "We were going to come over and say hello, but Roger's been a little under the weather. Won't you come in?"

The woman was tiny and wizened, face wrinkled soft and crepey, hair white and pulled back in a tight bun. She wore a navy cardigan over a blue floral housedress. As she held the door for Laura, her hand shook.

Laura forced a smile. "Of course," she said, as she followed the old woman inside.

She closed the door slowly behind herself, looking carefully around the house.

It was the mirror-image of their own, the same staircase, the same hook-wall, but the entrance to the living room was on the other side of the entry hall.

Everything was dirty, though. No, not dirty: old. Lived in. The house seemed tattered and worn, the paint flat and chipped, the floors dull, dust in the corners. Every surface was crammed with chintz and knickknacks, stacks of books and magazines on the end of each of the lower stairs.

It took Laura a moment to realize what was wrong. What was missing.

"You don't have any children?"

The old woman looked at her, wrinkling her eyes. "There haven't been children in this house in . . . my . . . sixty years?" She smiled, but there was something tight and wiry under her soft, wrinkled skin. "Are you all right, dear? You look—"

"I'm fine," Laura said quickly, glancing around the room, trying to make things make sense. "I just thought. . . ."

"How far along are you, dear?" the old woman asked, looking at her belly.

"Seven months," she said, curling her arm around the bump. "Almost."

"That's lovely," the old woman said, her smile just as pinched. "Would you like to—"

"There are no children here?" she asked again, looking for any sign: tiny boots, bottles on the side-board, small snow-jackets hung on the coat-hooks.

The old woman's eyes narrowed. "Dear, why do you keep asking that?"

She took a step toward the staircase, her eyes flicking from side to side, scouring the room. "I just thought. . . . Ever since we moved in, I thought I heard a baby crying. At night, mostly . . ."

The old woman drew in a sharp breath. "You've heard it too?"

Laura's whole body sagged in relief, her face breaking close to tears. "Oh my God. You've heard it? I thought—"

"It's the wind, dear," the old woman said, her smile sliding into something sadder, pitying.

"It's not—"

The woman reached out and laid her hand on Laura's arm, squeezing gently. It was probably supposed to be comforting, but her fingers were cold, bony and hard. "It's just the wind," she repeated, her voice now so sweet it was almost acidic. "I've been hearing it for a long time."

Laura seemed to fold back into herself. "How long?"

"Oh, years." She tilted her head, as if trying to remember an exact date. "I was terrified the first time I heard it, but it's just the wind. It's an old house."

Laura nodded deeply. Her breathing was slowing.

Just the wind.

"Oh goodness," the old woman said. "You've really had quite the fright, haven't you?" She squeezed her arm. "Did you really think it was ghosts?" She smiled widely. "It's all right. The boys aren't real."

Laura took a step back, pushing the old woman's hand off her arm, her eyes widening. "I didn't say anything about ghosts."

The old woman stepped toward her, her smile disappearing into the worn hardness of her face.

"Or boys," Laura whispered. "I didn't say anything about boys."

This time, the woman's smile bared her yellowing teeth. "Of course you did, dear," she said sweetly. "You said you had been hearing things. Boys."

"No," Laura said, certain. "I said baby. You said boys—"

"No," the old woman said, taking another step toward Laura. "You said—"

"I said baby!" Laura screamed. "I said baby." And then she broke altogether, her chest heaving, tears on her cheeks. "You said boys. Why did you say boys? Why did—"

"Get out," the old woman said flatly.

"—you say boys? And ghosts. Why—"

"Get out of my house." The old woman pushed on her shoulder, and Laura was surprised at her strength, like coiled wire inside a fading pillowcase. She stumbled back a step.

"Get out!"

Not even sure how it happened, Laura found herself on the porch, the door slamming in her face.

"What did you do?" she cried out, pounding her hands against the glass at the top of the door. "What did you do to those boys?"

She could see movement through the curtains. The old woman was still standing there, watching her. "What did you do?"

"Get off my porch," the woman yelled. "Or I'll call the police."

Laura leaned forward, pounded harder. "What did you do? What did you do?"

Meeting the woman's eyes a final time, Laura stumbled away. It was only a few steps to the front door, a short moment of fumbling for the key. What had the old woman done?

It took all of her strength, all of her weight, to push open the front door.

She almost fell into the foyer, and stopped short, clutching at the doorknob to keep her feet.

There was a little boy standing at the foot of the stairs.

He wasn't more than six or seven, tiny and blond, dressed in a pair of denim overall shorts and a white collared shirt. His feet were bare, and he jerked in surprise as Laura burst through the door.

"Who—" She couldn't form the words.

His eyes flashed, and he ran almost straight toward her, veering off at the last moment and disappearing behind the door, into the soft shadows of the hanging coats.

Laura shut the door gently, careful not to startle him.

"It's all right," she said, stepping toward the coat-hooks. "It's okay. I'm not going to hurt you."

She began taking coats off the hooks, casting them on the floor behind her, whispering the whole time. "Shh. It's all right. I want to help you. Shh."

She was careful not to make any sudden movements, lifting each coat slowly, carefully away.

"It's okay," she cooed. He must be so scared. "It's all right."

With each coat, she expected to see him, and the awareness started to rise within her as she thinned the hooks, but she refused to believe it until Curt's heavy wool coat hit the floor: he wasn't there.

There were just a couple of light jackets left, nowhere for even that little a boy to be hiding.

He wasn't there.

She dragged all the remaining jackets off the hooks with one sweep of her arm.

He wasn't there.

She sagged against the wall, bracing herself to keep from falling as waves of nausea and exhaustion rose up in her. When had she last eaten? When had she last slept?

But none of that mattered. Where was he? Where could he have gone?

The wall was cool and rough under her hand.

The wall . . .

Straightening up, she ran her hands slowly over the grainy surface. Was the wall too warm? Too cool? Something about it didn't feel quite right.

Had the boy disappeared into the wall?

But that was—

Something caught the edge of her hand, and she stopped, leaned forward.

It was a slightly raised crack in the plaster, with a thin layer lifting away from the surface underneath. She picked at it with her fingernail, and it flaked off, a hardened fleck of paint about the size of a dime that fell silently to the floor.

She slid her fingernail into the crack itself, pushing it as deep as it would go, then bent her finger, trying to hook deeper. Something had to open. There had to be something. She bit her lip as she pried at the wall, her fingernail splitting, tearing off.

She looked at the bleeding tip of her finger dumbly for a moment, then put it into her mouth, the taste of her own blood sharp and metallic on her tongue.

She needed something stronger. A knife maybe.

No, a hammer.

And then she remembered the short crowbar in Curt's pristine toolkit, on the shelf by the back door. That would work.

As she turned toward the kitchen, the boy was standing at the foot of the stairs again.

This time, he didn't run. He smiled at her, almost shyly, before turning away and climbing carefully onto the bottom stair.

"Wait!" Laura called, starting after him. The room shimmered and wavered around her, and she had to fight to keep her balance. "I just want to talk to you."

He stopped on the third step and turned to look at her. He

waited until she had reached the bottom step, until she had lifted her foot to step up, before he turned and continued climbing the stairs.

"Stop," she begged, stepping unsteadily up the stairs. "I just want—"

He stopped a half dozen steps away and turned, smiling so beatifically Laura almost gasped, a tiny hand clutching around her heart. He bounced on his feet as if he could barely suppress his forward motion, like he was excited to be leading her, at the prospect of showing her something.

"Are you taking me to the baby?" Every step seemed higher than the last, every lifting of her feet slower, more tentative. "Is that what you want to show me?"

His smile broadened and he skipped up the next few stairs.

"I'm coming," she said weakly the next time he turned around. She was almost pulling herself up the stairs by the banister, her head swimming, her shirt soaked with sweat.

This time he waited until she was only a couple of steps away before turning and starting upward again.

The next time, he was only two stairs away before he turned. Almost close enough to touch. Almost close enough to take his hand.

She grew weaker with every stair. She had to stop several times to close her eyes and take deep breaths to fight the dizziness, the swaying of the staircase.

She'd call an ambulance from the bedroom phone. It had gone too far. She needed to eat. She needed to sleep. Once she found the baby. . . .

It wasn't far now. A few more steps.

She was right behind the boy when he stopped at the top of the stairs, when he turned to her for the last time. He lifted his hand toward her. She felt the slightest pressure against her belly.

She flinched.

The loose board shifted under feet.

She tried to steady herself, tried to hang onto the railing as she felt herself starting to fall backwards.

Her arm twisted as she clung to the railing, as her body half-turned. Weak, and with the extra weight, there was no way she could stop herself. Her arm popped at the shoulder. She screamed, and let go.

Her body thundered down the stairs, turning and twisting as she tried in vain to curl herself around her belly, her head bouncing off several of the balusters as she tumbled.

She did all she could to save herself, to roll rather than fall, but three steps from the bottom of the staircase she hit her head first, the weight of her body crushing down on it, snapping her neck before she came to rest, splayed over the bottom stairs.

And then there was nothing: no light, no dark, no sound, no time. Not even the sense of distance, of comfort, that accompanies the deepest of sleeps, the darkest of nights.

Nothing.

The world returned with a wave of noise and a slap of cold, Laura shivering in the foyer, staring down at her body on the bottom steps. She wrapped her arms around herself, but she couldn't look away.

Her eyes were open, wide and blue, looking sightlessly toward the ceiling. They began to mist over, to dull. Her head was almost parallel to her shoulder, her neck distended and twisted. One arm was tight against her belly.

Without thinking, she slipped her hand down, over the rise of her abdomen. She waited a long moment, until she felt the baby kick. She rubbed her belly, and she half-smiled, and felt the tears burn in her eyes as she looked at the body at her feet. If her baby was kicking. . . .

She stared at the hand on the body's stomach. She hadn't been able to save the baby.

But it was with her. Always.

Always?

Her hand stopped.

She had died. *They* had died.

It wasn't a surprise, or a shock, simply a state of being. She was. They were.

She didn't hurt. Her mind was clear. She was cold, but she was beginning to get used to it. She felt a tugging inside herself, a feeling of emptiness, of longing, but she suspected she would get used to that, too.

Mostly, she was aware, more than she had ever been before. Everything had changed.

It wasn't just the recognition of her own body at her feet, the greying of her eyes. She had woken into this new world, this new awareness, knowing somehow. Knowing more, than she had.

She knew that the roaring she was hearing was the sound of the furnace, a distant hum once, now echoing through the house, her ears suddenly keen, and almost overwhelmed. She knew that she could see more clearly, as if all her senses had suddenly been reborn, free of decades of wear and disintegration.

And she knew that the little boy—

She looked toward the top of the stairs.

His face was tight and drawn, his mouth turned down, his eyes frantic, as if he were on the verge of tears.

"It's okay," she said, quietly and calmly. "I know you didn't mean to hurt me."

He took a step back from the top stair.

"It's all right," she said, taking a step toward him. "It's okay." Another.

He pressed his hand to his mouth, biting between his thumb and forefinger, as she approached him, eyes tightening, but he didn't step away.

"I know you didn't mean to hurt us," she said, as she came to the third step from the top. "It's all right." She extended her hand. "Is there something you wanted to show me?"

The boy hesitated, then nodded. His eyes were locked on her hand.

"All right," she said. She wiggled her fingers.

The loose step didn't move under her foot.

When he reached out, she closed her hand around his. It felt as if there were nothing there—no warmth, no weight—but there was a definite presence, a sense of his fingers, a sense of him, a sense of connection.

It was . . . it took her a long moment to figure it out.

Comforting. It was comforting.

"All right," she said again, and he led her toward the bedroom.

Seeing their home from this side—the other side, she thought—was like seeing it through someone else's eyes. The hallway seemed narrow, and dim, the bedroom small and cluttered and grey, somehow, as if she were seeing it through a screen.

But something about it pulled at her, the empty hollow within her surging as she looked at the bed, the covers thrown back, the pillows still bearing the imprint of their heads.

She stopped. For a moment, it was like she could smell Curt in the air, the warm damp of him fresh out of the shower, faint soapiness.

Curt . . .

Her heart turned in her chest. Curt was going to be devastated.

She could picture him at the breakfast table, a half grapefruit in front of him, a single coffee cup. She could picture him in their bed, still on his side, his arm across the emptiness beside him.

For the first time, she wanted to cry.

The boy pulled at her hand, and she turned away from the bed.

He led her to the corner of the room, the corner closest to the neighbour's, the corner where she had first heard the crying.

"Here?" she asked, when he stopped. "What did you want to—"

The boy stepped into the wall, disappearing into the plaster. Laura watched as her own arm slid through the eggshell surface, then she was stepping through.

The space behind the plaster was dark and narrow, less than eight inches deep before the backside of the neighbouring wall, hemmed by timber studs two feet apart, grey and dusty with age. There was no insulation, no wiring, just the cramped confines.

The boy's grip tightened.

"Oh my God."

The boy's body was pressed against the back of their neighbour's wall, hands extended above its head, the flesh dried away, leaving desiccated sticks, wrapped in grey, leathered skin. At the tips of its fingers, the nails had peeled back, bones poking through the fingertips, each dug into the wall in matching trenches. The mouth was pulled open in what looked like a never-ending scream, the hollow dark and black, the baby teeth still white, still shiny.

And Laura knew. She could see it all. The woman next door pushing the boy into the wall, holding him there while her husband plastered over the opening, his fingertips digging into the wet plaster as he screamed.

As they screamed.

At the body's feet was a small bundle, wrapped in white that had turned black in the decades it had been there, the opening at the top revealing the shrunken, leather face of the baby, eyes forever shut, mouth forever wide.

A baby.

Crying.

And she knew.

Releasing the boy's hand, Laura reached down, reached into the bundle of fragile twigs, and lifted the baby free of its mummified body, drew it close to her, where it squirmed and cried for a moment before settling, before nuzzling into her.

She cupped her hand under the baby's head, leaned close, brushed her lips against the tender of its scalp, the soft fuzz of its hair.

When she looked at the boy, he was smiling. Sad, but smiling.

Adjusting her grip on the baby, she reached down and took the boy's hand.

In the distance, she heard the front door opening, Curt's voice crying out in the empty house.

"It's going to be okay," she whispered, but she wasn't sure if she was telling the boy, or herself.

She blinked, and they were back in the foyer, she and the baby in her arms, the boy's hand still in hers.

Curt was crouched over her body, his face twisted into an anguished rage as he screamed, as he shook her shoulders. In her stomach, the tugging that had brought her to him pulled her closer, closer, until she was near enough to reach out for him.

Instead, she whispered, "Curt? Curt?"

But he didn't seem to hear. Not yet.

"Laura!"

All she wanted was to soothe him, to tell him it would be all right. To tell him they could be together. They could be a family, together.

She squeezed the boy's hand.

She would wait. In the dark, she would call for him. In the night silence, he would hear. He would come for her. He always came for her. It was one of the things she loved about him.

And then he would be here, and they would be together.

Forever.

THREE DAYS GONE

Martin was there in the park the day his brother Andrew disappeared. The newspapers all said so, and he was there in the grainy television footage, still in his baseball uniform, all gawky planes and obtuse angles. He was there. Everyone knew, but no one seemed to remember.

Everyone knew exactly what Andrew had been wearing. Everyone could picture him in their minds, although no one had actually seen him in the green pants and the blue Spider-Man t-shirt. Everyone had that last image of Andrew seared into their minds.

In disappearing, Andrew had come to life, had become a permanent fixture in the minds and hearts and souls of an entire community. An entire city. An entire province.

By not having vanished, by being around, Martin seemed to disappear.

{

The videotape footage is difficult to watch: hyper-saturated with colour, blurry and seemingly out of focus. It's a result of age and expectation: in its day, the camera would have been state of the art.

The date code in the corner of the footage reads 5.25.86.

The voice off-camera is quiet and kind, handling him with the softest of kid gloves. It's a television interview, but it hardly matters: when the police talked to him, they asked the same questions, and used the same gentle tones.

"And then what happened?"

In the video, Martin is skinny, his narrow face puffed and red from crying. His baseball uniform is grey, and has the logo of a local grocery store on the chest. He's wearing his ball cap, but he has it pushed back on his head.

"I went up to bat." He stammers a little when he talks, and his voice is thick with crying. "It was a double." For a moment he seems proud.

"Did you see your brother?"

He nods his head slowly. "He was at the fence, watching me, as I walked up to the plate."

"And then what happened?"

"Billy . . . Bill Carpenter . . . he was up next. He got a homer. I scored a run. . . ." His voice drifts off.

"Did you see Andrew, after that?"

He shakes his head, not even trying to speak.

"Did you see anything unusual in the park? Did you see anyone who seemed unusual? Anyone who you thought . . . Anyone who seemed out of place?"

Martin shakes his head again.

The gesture is a lie. He knows that if he opens his mouth to try to answer, he will give everything away.

{

It's a long road, Martin thought to himself. A long road that brings you home.

The face in the mirror was no longer that of the boy in the videotape. The boy, broken and fragile, was still in there, buried deeply, but there was little to give him away.

Martin Corbett was no longer what anyone would call skinny. His body was tight and compact, wiry and strong. His face was lean and hard, his eyes small. He seemed to carry himself with a fraught tension, a tightly coiled force barely contained by the blue shirt, the jeans.

"I'm gonna go out," he had told his mother a few minutes before.

She had looked at him, alarmed. "Are you sure?"

She was sitting at the kitchen table, a copy of the morning paper in front of her, open to the story about the anniversary of Andrew's disappearance. It was short, and buried near the back of the B section. Twenty-first anniversaries didn't seem to carry a lot of significance.

"I'm sure."

She reached for the glass in front of her before realizing—or remembering—that it was empty. "You know what—"

He cut her off. "I know the rules. No bars. No pubs. No drinking. No drugs." He tried to smile, tried not to notice how desperately she was looking at that empty glass. Trying not to look like she was looking. "I just need to get out of the house for a while, go for a walk or something. I've been cooped up here all day."

He didn't mention that it had been her that had done the cooping, insisting that they spend the afternoon looking at the photo albums, talking about Andrew. *"Sharing."* An afternoon of painful memories, punctuated by her regular trips to the kitchen for glasses of orange juice that, as the day wore on, grew increasingly pale.

"If I don't get out for a bit, I'll go crazy. Don't worry. I'll be careful. I won't get into any trouble."

Neither of them believed this entirely, but it was just one of the polite fictions they both observed.

She didn't even wait until he had closed the bathroom door before she was back at the fridge. She opened the freezer first, the neck of the vodka bottle kissing gently against the rim of the tumbler.

{

After the game, Martin had gone looking for his brother. At first, it had been impossible to see anything with everyone milling around: players whooping and shouting and running, line-ups at the concession stand, parents waiting to pick up their kids.

After a while, though, it had started to thin out. Martin couldn't find Andrew anywhere.

He didn't panic as he walked over to another area of the park, to the playground where Andrew spent most of his time, giggling down the slide or spinning on the roundabout.

He wasn't there.

Martin didn't panic as he walked back to the apartment. Andrew had probably just got bored and gone home: it had happened before. There would be hell to pay for Martin if that's what had happened.

It wasn't: Andrew wasn't at home.

But Martin didn't panic. Not even when his mother pushed the baby into his arms and ran out of the house, back to the park to look for her younger son. Not when she came back, flushed and red and choking back tears, reaching for the telephone to call the police.

Martin didn't panic until three days had passed. And by then it was far, far too late.

(

Did you see anyone unusual? Anyone you thought . . .

(

Martin had just lathered up his face when there was a soft knocking at the door. Too soft to be his mother, who usually pounded.

"Come in," he said, flicking the plastic sleeve off a disposable razor.

Tessa opened the door a crack and slid into the bathroom. "Mom's hard at it," she said, once the door was safely closed again.

"I don't think we're supposed to notice," he said, rinsing the razor under the hot water.

Tessa snorted. "Right. Like all the neighbourhood bums don't just wait for her to put the garbage out so they can get the bottles."

"And buy bottles of their own," he said. "The alcoholic circle of life."

She smiled. She was a pretty girl when she smiled. Martin didn't think it happened that often.

"It's hard," Tessa said, after a long moment. "Seeing her like this."

Martin shrugged. "It's the anniversary. You know how she gets."

Tessa shook her head. "It's getting worse. It used to be just the anniversary. Christmas. Andy's birthday. But lately . . ."

"What do you know about it?" he snapped. "You don't even live in the city anymore. You've got school. Your own apartment. Your own life."

"Who do you think she calls in the middle of the night, so pissed she can barely dial? It's sure as hell not you. Did they even allow you to get phone calls?"

He ignored the comment, watched the grey, stubbly shaving foam slip into the drain. "She calls?"

Tessa nodded. "Three or four times a week."

"What does she talk about?"

Tessa raised a disbelieving eyebrow.

"Right. Of course."

"Does she ever talk about anything else?"

Not as long as Martin could remember. "Is there anything in particular?"

"The usual stuff. How she was a terrible mother. How she spent too much time with me. How she never should have trusted you."

"The usual stuff," he echoed.

"Yeah. She's been talking about you a lot lately. Since you told her you were coming home."

"Yeah?"

"Yeah." She saw that he was waiting for something more. "More of the same. She talked a lot about you getting out. A lot about *The Day*. What you did. How you reacted."

"How I reacted?"

Tessa shrugged. "She said it was weird. Like you didn't react at all to him being gone. Like you weren't worried. At all. Like—" She stopped herself.

"What?"

"Nothing."

He took a last swipe with the razor. "Seriously. What?"

"It's just . . . she said at one point, one night when she was so hammered I could barely understand what she was saying, she said that she wondered, sometimes. . . . Given everything that happened after, she wondered—"

"She thought I had something to do with it."

Tessa looked at him, then nodded slowly. "Or that you knew more than you were saying."

"Right," he said, rubbing his hand lightly over the slick wet of his face, feeling for roughness.

"I don't think she meant—"

"Oh, she meant it all right," he said, still touching his face. He thought of adding "And she's not far wrong," but he didn't.

{

Martin and Andrew had always been close, closer than most brothers. Even with four years separating them, they stuck together. All the moves, the new apartments, the new kids in the neighbourhood; they stood together in the face of the seemingly unending changes.

After four new schools in less than four years, it looked like Victoria might become something resembling a hometown for the boys. Their mother had a new boyfriend, a new job. They moved into an apartment near downtown, and there was little of the usual feeling of impermanence, their tendency to live out of boxes and bags that had dogged their last few places. Their mother put pictures up on the walls; her boyfriend bought her a new rocking chair.

Martin and Andrew walked to and from school together, and in the afternoons Martin looked after his little brother until their mother got home from work. They spent the time playing on their old Atari, or watching the Fun-a-Rama cartoons on channel twelve. When their mother asked what they had been up to, they would both answer "Homework."

And then she got pregnant with Tessa and everything changed.

Her boyfriend claimed to be happy, but Martin and Andrew came home from school one afternoon to find his stuff gone from the apartment, and no sign of him. They had waited in silence for their mother to get home—no games, no cartoons today.

She didn't say anything, stepped into her bedroom and closed the door. Martin made mac and cheese for dinner.

They moved to a smaller apartment. A new school. No pictures on the walls.

After Tessa was born, it was like they had lost their mother. She didn't go to work anymore, and seemed to spend her days in the rocking chair, holding the new baby.

They would come home from school and she would flinch at the closing of the apartment door, at the sound of their voices.

When Andrew turned on the television, she would say, "Don't you have homework to do?"

He glanced at Martin. "It's done already."

The sound of cartoons filled the small room, and their mother pressed her eyes shut, as if in pain.

"Why don't you both go play in your room? Or, Martin, why don't you take your brother outside for a little while? Maybe the playground at the end of the block? Just 'til dinner time?"

"But I've got—" He was about to say "homework," but the expression on his mother's face seemed to hold no patience, no understanding. "Come on," he said to his brother, thinking about the TV shows he'd have to miss to finish his schoolwork after dinner.

After a few afternoons like that, they stopped even coming home after school. They'd hang out in the schoolyard or park with the kids who happened to be hanging around, waiting out the hours until the moment when the group seemed to dissipate all at once, responding to some unheard dinner call.

For the first while, their mother would have dinner waiting for them when they got home, Tessa burbling away in her bassinet. It was never very extravagant, but it was hot and filling and the three of them ate sitting together around the table that had followed them from apartment to apartment.

After a while, though, even those moments of togetherness disappeared.

They came into the apartment one evening to find the place

cold, and shrouded in shadows. The only sound was the creaking of the rocking chair.

"Mom?" Martin called out.

She didn't answer, and for a moment he thought she might have fallen asleep. But as he got closer to her he saw that her eyes were open, unfocussed, staring blankly out into the room.

"Mom? Are you okay?"

His voice seemed to surprise her and she blinked several times, coming back to herself. Almost.

"Mom?"

"I—I'm okay. I guess I got a little distracted." She seemed flustered, confused. Tessa stirred in her arms. "Are you hungry, little girl?" she cooed.

"I'm hungry," Andrew said, and Martin shot him a look.

Their mother didn't seem to notice, tugging up her shirt to feed her sister.

Martin waited a long, silent moment. Waited for their mother to say something about dinner, to say anything. To remember that they were there.

"Come on," he said, when it was clear that no words were going to come. "I'll make you a grilled cheese sandwich."

Andrew's smile seemed to brighten the room. "I'll help," he said.

Tessa followed him from the bathroom into his old bedroom, the one next door to Andy's room. His mother had turned Martin's room into a guest room while he was away—it had all the character of a cheap hotel room, with a painting of Jesus centred over the head of the bed. *There's absolutely no trace of me here*, Martin had thought to himself when he first walked through the door. Good. He preferred it that way. He didn't bother to unpack his duffel bag. It was fine to feel like a guest. Better that way, even. He had no desire to come home, despite all that he had said.

"So you're going out?" Tessa said.

"Yup." He put his razor and shaving cream on the small dresser, next to his toothbrush and watch.

"Where you goin'?"

"Just for a walk."

"Are you sure?"

Something in her tone—her blatant disbelief, perhaps—made him look at her face, to see the same doubts there.

"Did Mom send you to ask me that?"

"No," she said, a little too loudly.

"Right."

He shook his head.

"Fuck," he muttered, tugging his t-shirt off, hoping that she would get the message that it was time to give him some privacy. Time to get the hell out.

She didn't take the hint. "They can do testing any time they want, you know. Unannounced. They just show up. They find out you've got anything in your system, you go—"

"Jesus, do you think I'm stupid? Do you think I spent all that time getting out just to get sent back? Shit, if I wanted to get high, prison would be the easiest place to do it."

He thought he might have been too loud, too strident, but she didn't flinch. "So where are you going?"

"Like I told Mom, I need some air. I need to get out of here, just for a while."

He crouched down, fumbled in his duffel bag for a clean black t-shirt. When he straightened up and turned back around, his sister was staring at him, her mouth open, her calm façade a memory.

"What—" She couldn't even form the question.

He knew what she was going to ask. "The scar?" He turned his head, craning his neck as if trying to look at his own back. "How's it look? I hear it's pretty impressive, but I've never seen it for myself."

"How . . ."

"I *told* them it was self-defence," he said, then lifted his hands, palms up, as if to shrug. "I would have thought a fourteen-inch wound on my back was pretty compelling evidence."

If you had asked him, Martin would never have said that he minded looking after his younger brother. It wasn't just a matter of 'everyone pitching in and pulling their weight' as their mother used to say. He genuinely liked spending the time with Andrew. They had a lot of fun, and the explorations and discoveries transformed their few blocks—a rough area surrounding the ugly block of subsidized housing they had moved into—from a strange wasteland into something of a neighbourhood.

He did like that he had baseball to himself, though.

Tuesdays and Thursdays Martin made dinner early, made sure that Andrew ate quickly and got settled into something in his room—something quiet, something that wouldn't disturb their mother, that wouldn't wake their sister—before changing into his uniform and running out the door, calling over his shoulder, "I've got practice. I'll be back."

He was always late to the diamond, but Coach Phillips never said anything about it, just dropped him into whatever drill the team was running.

For a few weeks they just practiced, but once the league started up they played at least three games a week, Tuesday and Thursday nights, and Saturday afternoons.

Martin loved to play. He was a good fielder, and he settled comfortably into shortstop. He had good instincts, and a keen sense for the game as it unfolded, an ability to keep the field and the players in his mind like chess pieces on a board. He was a strong hitter, and his numbers kept him near the top of the league stats.

While this all certainly added to his enthusiasm for the game, they were not the reason for his love of it. What he loved was the chance to be with his friends, to hang out with Billy in the dugout, to be working together to eke out a win. More than anything else, though, he loved being able to disappear into something for a few hours on a spring evening or afternoon, to live entirely in those moments, not thinking about anything else.

For a few hours each week, he could just *be*.

That all changed when he got home late one Thursday night.

The game had gone long—a hard-fought battle with their closest rivals. They had won by a single run, Martin's run, a late-inning homer that had sailed over the midfield fence, bouncing white in the parking lot. His teammates, his friends, had hoisted him on their shoulders and carried him around the infield. The coach slapped him on the back, offered to buy everyone ice cream to celebrate.

Normally Martin would have bowed out, slipping away in the post-game confusion and heading for home. But this was his night, and when the coach looked at him and asked, "You coming?" he had nodded.

The whole time they were celebrating, though, all Martin could think about was how thrilled his mother was going to be when she heard about the game-winning run, and how he wished she had been at the game to see it for herself.

He practically ran home, throwing open the main door of the building, taking the stairs two at a time.

He stopped dead outside their apartment, key at the ready, hand extended. From behind the door he could hear Tessa wailing, the deep, throaty roar she got when she had been crying for a long time, and his mother's shaking voice. A door slammed.

He fumbled the key into the lock and opened the door slowly. "Mom?" he called out.

She was screaming as he came around the corner into the living room. "Where have you been? Where did you go?" Her face was bright red, her eyes wide and bright, her hair a tangled mess. She was holding Tessa, her upper body lurching as if that might quiet the screaming child. "Where were you?"

Martin flinched under the force of the words. He had never seen her like this.

"Where were you?" she asked again, stepping toward him.

"I was at baseball," he managed.

"Don't *lie* to me," she screamed. "I know when you're lying. I can tell. I can always tell."

Martin took a step back, into the doorway. "I was at baseball," he repeated, weakly.

She slapped his face. He could hear the sound of it before he felt the blow. It was so hard it snapped his head to one side, and left a vivid red handprint on his cheek.

"Mom—"

"Don't *lie* to me," she snarled. "You come in here from God knows where, telling me lies. . . ."

"Mom, I'm not—" He could feel the tears burning in his eyes, the pain radiating from the slap.

"You ungrateful little—"

Behind her, he could see the door to Andrew's room crack open, could see his brother peer out, his face stained with crying.

"You're as bad as your father."

"Mom—"

"I work so hard. I work so hard to make a home for you, and what do you do? Nothing. You waltz around here like a little prince, you come and go as you please, you never lift a finger to help out—"

"Mom!"

She raised her hand again and he shrank back. Andrew's bedroom door closed without a sound.

"I give and I give and I give and you do nothing but take. You're not a part of this family. You're a parasite. You suck up everything that's good—"

He didn't hear anymore—he couldn't bear to. Stepping all the way out into the hallway, he pulled the door shut and ran for the front door as fast as his legs would carry him.

He couldn't make out any of the words she screamed behind him. He turned the corner, pushed open the door, and was gone into the night.

❀

He closed the guest room door behind Tessa and stood for a moment just listening to the sound of his own breath, savouring the feeling of being alone for once, finally.

It didn't take him long to dress—he didn't have much in the way of clothes, and he had pretty much lived in jeans and a black t-shirt anyway. Before.

He sat on the bed to pull up his socks, to tie his Docs. As he ran the laces through the top couple of eyelets, he could feel the slow burning start within him, the cool, stony feeling of inevitability that would build and build until he gave it release.

He smiled.

It wasn't always like this. Sometimes the anger came too fast, too surprisingly, and he had no chance of controlling it. That's what had got him into trouble: those flashes of anger, the sudden bursts of fury that left him blind, almost devoid of memory of what he had done.

That's why he had spent all those years away.

But this, this feeling of cold fire in his belly, this was almost comforting, a familiar friend he knew he could count on. A feeling that had never let him down.

Standing up, he looked at himself in the mirror. Not at his face, not checking his shave or his hair, but meeting his own eyes in the cold glass, recognizing himself there. Centering himself. Steeling himself.

He tugged on his leather jacket, made sure his wallet and cigarettes were in the pockets, then nodded at his own reflection.

Before he left, he took one last look around the room that had once been his home. There were no details there to consign to memory, nothing to take with him, even knowing he wouldn't be back.

{

Martin ran to the playground at the end of the block, clutching his cheek as if he could touch his mother's hand there, as if he could pull the pain, the very action of the slap, away.

He didn't let himself cry until he was sitting in one of the swings.

How could she do that? How could she say those things? He tried so hard, and he thought . . .

His tears ran down his cheeks, collected at his chin before falling to the ground. His back buckled with the weight of his sobs.

He tried so hard. He did everything she asked. He took care of

Andrew. He made dinner. He did everything he could, didn't he? How could she say things like that? Why was she so angry? What had he done to make her so mad? To make her hit him?

He twisted in the swing, dragging the tops of his shoes in the sand.

What had he done wrong? What could he do better?

"Are you all right?"

Martin choked back his surprise, stopped spinning and looked up. He hadn't heard anyone coming, but there was someone there. A man.

"I'm sorry. I didn't mean to scare you." His voice was soft and gentle. "I saw you sitting here and I thought you might need some help."

"That's okay," Martin said, wiping his nose as he looked up at the man. "I'm all right."

The man crouched down, bringing himself to Martin's level. His hair was dark, almost black under the harsh yellow of the streetlight. His eyes were blue, and they seemed to look at him with a calm warmth and understanding. "It's a little late for you to be out here by yourself, crying, if you're all right."

"I'm okay," Martin said, less strongly.

"Are you sure?" the man asked. "You look like you could use someone to talk to."

Martin looked away, wiped at his nose again. The man was making him feel strange. His mother had warned him about talking to strangers, about some of the dangers boys faced at the hands of strange men. He knew better than to talk to him.

But he seemed so nice. His face was friendly and open; it looked like he might really care, like it might actually be good to talk to him.

Martin didn't know what to do.

The man cleared his throat. "I'm Jackson," he said, extending his hand. "Jack."

Martin took it carefully, shook it. "Martin."

"So what's going on, Martin?"

He shook his head, his resistance starting to crumble. "Nothing."

The man half-smiled. "Do your parents know that you're out

here by yourself? It's pretty late. They might be worried."

Martin shook his head just once, not saying anything.

"Ah. I see. What was the fight about?"

Martin looked at him sharply.

"You think I don't remember what it was like to be your age? Clearly there was some sort of fight. Most boys your age are tucked fast in their beds by now. But you're out here all by yourself."

"It's nothing," he repeated.

"Let me guess," the man said, sitting on the swing next to Martin's. "You got into a fight with your mom and dad—"

"Just mom. There's no dad."

"Ah. Well, that makes sense. You got into a fight with your mom and things got pretty hot and you came out here to cool off."

Martin didn't nod, didn't speak.

"So what was the fight about? Something you were supposed to do around the house? Something you *forgot* to do?"

"No," Martin snapped. "I do everything around the house. Everything. And she never—"

"She doesn't appreciate you."

"It's always Tessa this and Tessa that. She never puts her down. Carries her everywhere."

The man nodded as if he understood.

"And Andrew—Jesus. I walk him to school, I look after him after school, I cook him dinner and get him ready for bed. I hate it. There's never any time for me to do any of the things I want to do. I never get to have any fun." He didn't know where the words were coming from, and didn't know how true they were, even as he was speaking them, but they felt good to say, a hot rush of anger pushing out the sadness he had been feeling.

"It's hard being an older brother, isn't it?"

Martin nodded. "Sometimes."

The man leaned forward.

"I just wish I had a little more time for myself, you know? Like tonight. I know I came home late, but . . ."

"But you went out with your team."

Martin nodded, surprised that he would know this.

"You were celebrating. You scored the winning run."

"How do you—"

"What did your mom say when you told her about the game? About hitting the home run?"

Martin sank into himself.

"You didn't tell her."

He shook his head. "No," he whispered.

"Because of Tessa. And Andrew.

"She was so mad."

"Did she hit you?"

Martin's first response was to lie, to deny that the slap had happened, to deny that such a thing was even possible. But he nodded. Slowly.

"I thought so."

Martin felt like he might start crying again. He knew that if he spoke, it would be in tears, coming to his mother's defence. And he didn't want to do that.

"Does she hit your brother too?"

"Andrew?" He snorted a laugh. "No." As if it was the most ridiculous idea he had ever heard.

"That's not fair to you, is it?"

"None of it's fair."

"No, it's not. It's not easy being a big brother. Always having to be responsible. Always keeping an eye out. Never able to have any fun."

Martin felt himself nodding along as the stranger spoke.

"Never getting a chance to just be a kid yourself."

"Sometimes I wish he'd just disappear," Martin muttered, mostly to himself.

The stranger looked surprised. "You don't really mean that."

"Yes, I do." He didn't, but he didn't like the sceptical tone in Jack's voice.

"You think that everything would be better if Andrew wasn't around anymore?"

"Even for just a couple of days," he said, his voice threatening to break. "I could play baseball and hang out with my friends. I wouldn't have to worry about him making noise and bugging Mom. Even just a few days of not having to worry all the time."

"You think that three days without your brother would make everything better?"

Martin shrugged. "It couldn't make things worse."

The man smiled. "You should be careful what you wish for."

In the years he had been inside, Victoria had changed. It wasn't any single thing, but an accumulation of small changes that left Martin feeling like he was walking through a dream. The roughest hotel downtown, where he had spent many happy afternoons in the bar flying high and picking fights, had been turned into condominiums. The strip club he used to hang out at had turned into a pub, full of university students and hippies. There were no more hookers working along Government Street, and everywhere he turned there were coffee shops.

The city hadn't changed completely, though. It took him less than half an hour to get his bearings, to figure out where Tommy was likely to be.

Most people avoided that block of Pandora. The sidewalks were clear and wide, but as Martin walked past the old church, people stepped out of the shadows and stairwells.

"Smoke?"

"Crack?"

"X?"

"Got a little blow."

All of them young men, sunken-cheeked, with hoods pulled over their heads so only the lower halves of their faces were visible, their eyes gleaming in the shadows. They rolled when they walked, as if their joints were all too loose for proper coordination, and their pants sagged off their skeletal hips.

Martin shook his head to each question and kept walking, his eyes fixed on a small crowd across the street from the McDonald's.

Tommy stepped away from the ledge he had been leaning on when he saw Martin approaching, stepped through the crowd that parted easily for him, and stood there, shaking his head, a broad smile across his face.

"Well shit. If it ain't himself, back from the dead."

"Or something like that," Martin said, smiling. He extended a hand, but Tommy pulled him into his arms, slapping his back soundly. "Good to see you, man," he whispered into Martin's ear. He stepped back, surveying him. "I bet it feels good to be out."

"Oh, I dunno. I was starting to enjoy the group showers."

Tommy smirked, and a few of the people around them laughed. The small crowd had gathered close, sensing something important, something different, at last, happening.

"So you behave yourself in there?" he asked, leadingly, knowing the answer full well.

Martin shrugged. "I ran into some trouble. You know me."

"I know you."

The crowd began to drift away, already bored. One young guy, wearing a black marshmallow jacket over a stained white wifebeater, stayed close, rocking on his heels and staring at Martin.

"Who's this?" he asked, punching out the words. He had a long scar up one cheek, narrowly missing an eye before it disappeared into his hair-line. There was something familiar about him. Maybe his cold blue eyes, or the set of his jaw.

"This," Tommy started, already building extravagance in his voice. "Is my old friend Martin. Martin and me—" he shook his head "—we were legends when you were still pissing your pants."

The kid ignored the jab, focussing on Martin's face. "Martin Corbett?" he asked dismissively, as if he could barely be bothered to ask.

Martin nodded. "Why?"

"Heard you was in prison is all."

Martin didn't believe him, and it was clear that the kid didn't expect him to.

"I got out." Still searching for something in his face to confirm the familiarity he was feeling.

"It happens sometimes," Tommy said, looking between the two of them. "You wanna give us a minute, Marco? I think we've got some catching up to do, Martin and me."

Marco made a snorting, dismissive noise as he turned away, walking over to the rest of the group.

Martin watched him go, watched as he positioned himself so he could keep an eye on him and Tommy without looking like he was looking.

"How long you been back?" Tommy asked.

"Couple of days."

"How's your mom?"

Martin shrugged.

"Right. And Tessa?"

"She's living in Vancouver now, going to school." He waited a beat. "Criminology."

Tommy looked at him incredulously. "No shit?"

"No shit."

Tommy chuckled. "Well, you tell her I say hello the next time you're talking to her."

"Right."

Tommy slapped him on the shoulder, smiling like he might burst. "It's good to have you back."

"It's good to be out."

Tommy leaned in, lowered his voice. "You need anything, man? Little toot? Little smoke? Something to get your legs back under you? Maybe we oughta go out a little later, find us some girls?"

Martin was warmed by his old friend's obvious concern for him.

"I do need something," he said quietly.

"What do you need, man? Anything. Anything you need."

"I need a gun," Martin said simply. "Tonight. As soon as you can get it for me."

Tommy stepped back, his smile replaced with a thoughtful scowl. "Sure," he said. "No problem. It's gotta be tonight, though?"

Martin nodded. "Tonight. As soon as you can. There's someone I've got to meet."

❧

His heart was racing and he was a bit out of breath as he bounced on the bag. Second base. And now Billy was up to bat! He puffed a little air out from his cheeks, then glanced at the fence, keeping one eye on the pitcher.

Andrew saw him looking and waved. Martin nodded back and smiled at his little brother, then turned his full attention back to the pitch.

Everything at home seemed back to normal. By the time he had come in from the park his mother was in bed, and she hadn't said anything the next day.

When it was time for him to leave for his Saturday game, he had told Andrew to put on his shoes and coat.

"Where are we going?" he asked, pulling his attention away from the television.

"Baseball," he said.

Both of them glanced at their mother, but the conversation barely seemed to register with her.

"Okay," Andrew said, getting to his feet. Martin ruffled his hair as he walked past, and his brother pushed his hand away playfully.

The first pitch was a ball, and Billy stepped back from the plate, knocked the bat against his cleats, stretched, sighed. Martin glanced back at Andrew, who offered him a thumbs-up. He began to regret not bringing him to games before this: he seemed to be enjoying it, and it was kind of nice to have someone out there to cheer for him.

He watched the next pitch. Another ball, high and outside.

When he looked back at his brother, the man in the black leather jacket, the man from the park, was standing next to him, one hand on his shoulder. The man smiled when he saw Martin looking, then leaned over and whispered something in Andrew's ear.

Andrew smiled broadly, and they both waved to Martin.

Martin glanced away, his attention drawn instinctively back to the plate, where Billy swung big, digging deep for a pitch that sailed past him. Strike one.

When he looked back, the man—Jack—had straightened back up. Andrew waved again, but it wasn't an acknowledgement, or a greeting. He was waving goodbye, smiling. The man held up three fingers, meeting Martin's eye, made sure he saw. Three fingers.

They both turned and started to walk away, the man's hand back on Andrew's shoulder.

Andrew's name pushed its way up Martin's throat, but he held it back. He glanced around the field at the players from the other team. Took a step off the base, then back on. What could he do? He couldn't just leave. He couldn't yell: everyone would look at him. He couldn't—

Andrew and the man stopped, turned, and waved again at Martin.

The man raised his other hand, gesturing broadly at the air in front of him in a way that made Martin think of painting.

The slap of the ball into the catcher's mitt made Martin glance away. When he looked back, he watched as the man seemed to pull away a section of the world, a rectangular piece of the air falling away.

It looked like a doorway, hanging in nothing.

And from it spilled a light like Martin had never seen, a rich, golden glow that seemed more pure than sunset, but touched with green and blue, a warm bright that seemed to thrum in the air, to pull at him, drawing him toward it.

Martin felt suddenly like he was in a dark cave, had always been there, and now, nearing the surface, he was afforded a glimpse out at the world beyond, a world of light and warmth, a glimpse that made him realize how cold, how dark, the world around him really was.

Andrew and the man stepped into the doorway.

There was a crack of a bat against a ball and the crowd roared like a single voice, and when Martin looked back, his brother was gone. The man in the leather jacket was gone. The doorway was gone.

The light was gone.

꡴

He got himself a cup of coffee at the Starbucks at the corner of Government and Yates and sat at an outside table, smoking cigarettes and butting them out in the plastic lid from the coffee-cup.

Tommy had told him to meet him here, had told him to wait.

When he had asked how long, Tommy had just said, "Shouldn't be too long."

Martin hoped not. He glanced at his watch: it was getting late. Midnight coming on fast, and he wanted to be there ahead of time, waiting.

So much goddamned waiting.

Oh well. It probably wouldn't take Tommy too long. It never did in the old days.

The old days . . .

Martin marvelled at how much had changed in what felt like such a short time. The years he'd spent in prison had felt like a suspension of time—it surprised him to find that things had moved on, that everything had changed when he wasn't looking.

Like this coffee-shop. He remembered when it was a bookstore, remembered spending hours sitting on the floor with Tommy, both of them baked out of their minds, laughing their asses off to *Far Side* books and *Calvin & Hobbes*.

That was after they stopped playing baseball, after Andrew had disappeared, but back when it was still just the two of them. Back before things had started to go wrong.

{

At first, Martin wasn't worried when Andrew disappeared. For some reason, he felt like he could take Jack at his word. The man in the leather jacket had said three days when they had talked in the park. He had held up three fingers as he was leaving with Andrew. And something about that light, spilling in from the doorway he had drawn in the air, so warm. . . .

Martin trusted him.

And that feeling held out for three days. He waited, close by the door, the whole of that third day. Every time a policeman knocked, every time the phone rang, he knew, he just knew, that it was someone telling them that Andrew had been found.

But he wasn't. And lying in bed, watching midnight coming on, Martin knew, with a cold, sudden certainty, that he wouldn't be. His brother was gone.

Of course he couldn't say anything. He'd spent three days lying—to his mother, to the police, to the people from the TV and the newspaper—he couldn't come back now and tell them what he'd really seen, what he really knew. It's not like they would believe him.

He couldn't say anything. Hadn't he wanted Andrew to be gone? Wasn't that what he told Jack that first night in the park? It was all his fault, wasn't it?

He kept his silence while the search continued, through the days after the disappearance when it was like everyone in Victoria passed through their apartment, asking to help; through the days it seemed every telephone pole, every tree, every wall in the city had his brother's picture under the words "Have You Seen Andrew?" And then later, when the people stopped coming. When the newspaper stopped running stories. When the newscasters would end their short updates with sad shakes of their heads and weighty silences. When the posters yellowed and puckered in the damp, faded and, eventually, disappeared.

Martin kept his silence.

It wasn't hard. There was no one to talk to at home. His mother had come out of her darkness with Andrew's disappearance, but as time passed she disappeared again into her new role as professional mother, denier of the possibility that Andrew was truly gone. She took to wearing t-shirts printed with the same image from the posters, carrying the question "Have you seen Andrew?" everywhere she went. She kept Andrew's room exactly the way it had been the morning that he disappeared, and whenever she was interviewed, she insisted that it happen in his room. "We're keeping it just like this until he comes home," she would say. She carried Tessa with her everywhere, but she would barely meet Martin's eye when they passed in the apartment.

He didn't tell her that he had quit playing baseball; he never went back after Andrew left. His coach tried calling a few times, but Martin had hung up on him gently, and after a while he stopped trying. His mother never even noticed.

She didn't notice when he and Tommy started hanging out together, spending long afternoons in his room with the door closed. She didn't notice the towels wedged into the seam under the door, and if she noticed the smell of smoke on his clothes, she didn't say anything.

The first time he smoked pot it was with Tommy. They were in his room, listening to a Mötley Crüe tape and pretending to do homework when Tommy pulled a baggie out of his knapsack pocket.

"You wanna?"

"Sure." He didn't hesitate.

"So where'd you get it?" he asked as Tommy started to roll on the front cover of his science textbook. He already knew the answer.

"My brother," Tommy said, simply. There was no need for further explanation: Jimmy Connelly was infamous in the neighbourhood as a drug dealer, the sort of kid that parents warned their children to stay away from.

Most parents. Martin's mother hadn't said anything: she probably didn't even know who Jimmy Connelly was. And if she did, she clearly hadn't made the connection to Tommy.

"He says it's good stuff."

"Yeah?"

He fumbled with the paper. "That's what he says."

Martin watched him in silence. "Have you ever . . ." He cocked his head toward the small pile of weed.

Tommy puffed himself up like it was the most ridiculous question. "Oh yeah," he said, his voice louder than it needed to be. Then, as if remembering himself and who he was talking to, he seemed to deflate, and his voice lowered. "A couple of times. With my brother. He let me try it when he was hanging out with his friends. They thought it was pretty funny."

Martin waited, then prompted. "And?"

"And what?"

"What's it like?"

Tommy extended the finished joint toward him. "See for yourself."

At first, Martin didn't notice anything, too focussed on the burning of the smoke in his throat and struggling to suppress a coughing fit as he held the smoke inside him.

"What do you think?" Tommy asked, after they had passed the joint back and forth a couple of times.

Martin shook his head, not sure how to tell Tommy that he wasn't feeling anything.

"Nothing, eh?"

Martin smiled half-heartedly.

"You have to let yourself feel it," Tommy explained. "Here, lean back." Martin fell back against the pillow. "Try it again. This time, just let yourself feel it. Close your eyes and really feel it."

Martin took another toke and, passing the joint back to Tommy, let his eyelids droop shut. He could hear his pulse in his ears, feel the burning of the smoke in his lungs. And then he thought—no, he *could*—he could feel the blood in all of his arteries and veins, feel the heat and the motion of it in his chest, the prickly tingling of it in his fingertips. He could feel a rush pushing through him, a surge of warmth and ease, and something else. Potential. For a moment, he felt limitless, and when he breathed out the smoke, he could feel himself connecting to everything in the room, in the universe, a surging openness as if he were cracking slowly open, the light within him spilling out.

The light . . .

That was it. What he was feeling was like what he had felt at the ball diamond that day, that feeling of limitlessness, of comfort and ease and connectedness that he had felt when he saw the light from the open doorway. That's what this was like.

When he opened his eyes, he thought he saw it, just for a moment: a rich golden light that seemed alive, full of voices, of song, a light he could feel as much as see.

But then he blinked and it was just his room, with Tommy looking down at him, smiling and nodding. "I told you it was wicked."

Martin managed to smile, to conceal his disappointment at the loss of the light. Again.

He held out his hand for the joint.

❦

Martin checked his watch—8:15. He sighed, leaned back in his chair. His coffee cup was empty, but he lit another cigarette. They'd be chasing him off this table pretty soon.

Where the hell was Tommy?

Every person passing made him look up. Every sound of footsteps, every car idling at the light, caught his attention. He took a deep drag, trying to calm his nerves. Jagged. And the coffee wasn't helping.

Where the hell was he?

❦

Tommy had always been there for him. And he had always been there for Tommy—it went both ways. After a while it was like they were brothers, inseparable. They stayed over at each other's houses most nights, hung out at school together, cut classes together. When it was the two of them, nothing could stop them.

It was only when Martin was alone that things seemed to go wrong.

He was alone the night of the first anniversary of Andrew's disappearance. He had come home, still half-cut, to get a few hours' sleep, maybe a shower and a change of clothes.

His mother was waiting for him. She didn't even let him get into the apartment before she started in.

"Where have you been?" she screamed.

It was all too familiar. Martin glanced around the apartment as she stepping toward him, not catching his breath until he saw Tessa sitting on the living room floor, playing with the wooden blocks that used to be Andrew's.

"I was at Tommy's."

"Don't you lie to me," she snapped. "Sue just called here to see if there was anything we needed *today*." She emphasized the word, as if he might have overlooked its importance. "And to make sure that Tommy wasn't being a nuisance."

Martin shook his head, marvelling at how easily stories could fall apart.

"She was surprised when I said I thought both of you were over at her house."

"Huh." The sharp chuckle escaped from him before he could stop it.

She stepped forward, and he watched her hands, steeling himself, while she studied as his face.

"Are you high?" she asked in a voice not much more than a whisper. This close he could smell the fumes coming off her. Gin this time, it smelled like.

When he didn't answer, she repeated the question, more loudly. "Are you high right now?"

"I guess I come by it naturally," he said slowly, deliberately.

This time, the slap didn't surprise him, and he didn't wait around for her to be finished yelling at him.

He pushed past her, and as she was screaming about how he was grounded, how he wasn't allowed to see Tommy Connelly ever again, he stepped into his room and closed the door.

He sat at the edge of his bed, listening to her through the door, waiting for his heartbeat to slow down. He'd sleep for a while, he decided. And when he woke up, when he was ready to go out, she'd be out herself, collapsed at the table with her bottle of gin, Tessa put to bed before she let it get too far.

Until then . . .

He kicked off his shoes and laid down on the bed. From inside his cigarette pack he took out a flat plastic bag, slid a tab of acid under his tongue and closed his eyes, waiting for the light.

Tommy slid into the chair across from him without Martin ever hearing him coming. He smiled at his oldest friend, comforted by his mere presence, able to put the reason for their meeting out of his mind for the moment.

"I was starting to worry that you weren't going to show up," Martin said.

"I've never been hung up on punctuality or schedules," Tommy said. "Do you want a coffee?"

Martin looked to his empty cup and thought about declining, but he nodded. A little more caffeine might actually help later on.

Tommy tapped on the window and the kid in line—the kid with the scar, the one who couldn't stop staring at Martin—turned. Tommy raised two fingers and the kid nodded.

"You've got a butler now?"

Tommy laughed. "Just another kid from the neighbourhood. Probably thinks he'll get a handle on the business, steal some trade secrets from me then set himself up." He shook his head. "Marco. Marco Cezzoni."

Tommy reached into his pocket, pulled out his cigarettes and a lighter, and lit up without his eyes leaving Martin's face. Watching him. Waiting for his reaction. "I think you knew his brother."

Martin leaned forward, craning his neck to keep his eye on the kid through the window. That was why he had looked so familiar. Cezzoni. Fucking Rudy Cezzoni.

Tommy was still watching him intently. "I heard you messed him up pretty good."

Martin was sure that he was imagining the sudden burning and itching of the scar on his back. "He got me pretty good."

"I heard that, too."

The kid was paying for the coffees, then he disappeared around the corner, out of sight, toward the cream and sugar.

"But you got your own back, right? And then some. Word is it was you that killed him. Beat him so bad they weren't even sure whose body they had found. But they couldn't pin it on you."

Martin didn't say anything to disabuse him of the notion. He was enjoying the smile on Tommy's face, the quiet admiration in his friend's eyes. "That was another time. Another place."

"You never did take any shit from anybody."

"That'll be on my tombstone," he said, trying to sound dramatic. "Might also explain why I've spent so much time inside, too."

They both laughed, stopping only when the kid arrived with their coffees. He served Tommy first, setting the cup carefully in front of him, then repeated the process for Martin. Martin watched: the kid never looked at him, never let on that there was anything between them. Completely calm, completely cool.

Too calm. Too cool.

No way was he drinking that coffee.

The kid walked to the corner of the building, leaned near the door, and lit a cigarette.

"Is this," Martin gestured toward Marco, "going to be a problem?"

Tommy looked down the wall at him. "Marco? Nah. He knows that you and me go back, that there's history there. He knows better than to fuck with that." He peeled the plastic cover off his cup and took a drink.

"Blood runs pretty deep."

"He knows better." Tommy's tone was flat, certain, allowing for no further discussion.

"So why do you need a gun?" he asked without warning, the abrupt change of topic taking Martin by surprise.

"I told you. There's someone I've got to meet."

"And you need the gun for protection?" He left the question open.

Martin didn't answer.

"That's what I thought."

"I can get you some money in the next couple of . . ."

Tommy held up a hand. "Don't."

Martin nodded. "All right. Thanks."

Tommy shrugged. "I got as clean as I could get on short notice. No history, near as I can tell. The serial is filed off, but. . . ."

Martin felt a strange relief come over him. He hadn't even known that he'd been worrying. "Thanks. I appreciate that."

"It runs pretty deep, too, you and me."

"Yeah."

"Do you need anything else? I got—I got whatever you want. You know that. A little blow? A little crank? A little weed to take the edge off?"

It took Martin a moment to shake his head, his uncertainty surprising him.

"All right," Tommy said as he stood up. "I'm gonna hit the

head, then hit the road." He extended his hand. "Good seeing you, Martin."

Martin stood up and pulled his friend into an embrace. They held it for a moment, then slapped each other heartily on the back before releasing it.

"Stay out of trouble, Martin," he said, turning toward the door. "Or get yourself out of it clean."

As Tommy disappeared into the coffee shop, Martin sat back down to wait, staring at the full cup of coffee in front of him.

When he looked up toward Marco, he caught the kid looking away. Not too cool. Not too cool at all.

{

Waking up in the dark prison infirmary, Martin knew that he wasn't alone. A cold fear cut through the morphine haze—his first thought was of Rudy, come to finish the job. He tried to pull himself to a sitting position, to figure out some way to defend himself, but the movement was too much, and he could feel the cut across his back like a line of fire against his skin.

It wouldn't be a fair fight, then. He didn't think that would worry Rudy too much.

"You keep jumping around like that you're going to pull out all your stitches," came a voice from the darkness. "Just relax. You've got nothing to fear from me."

The voice was vaguely, distantly familiar. Martin struggled to make out the figure in the darkness, through the morphine cloud in front of his eyes. "Who . . ."

Without warning, a light came on. Martin didn't know from where, but he flinched from the brightness. It took his eyes a moment to adjust.

The man in black was sitting in a chair alongside his bed.

Jack. The man from the park. The man who had taken Andrew.

"You—" Martin struggled again, trying to rise, the surge of fury almost overcoming the pain. Almost.

The man shook his head. "I told you—you're going to pull out your stitches." His voice was even, unconcerned.

He was exactly as Martin remembered him: the same face, the same jacket, the same faintly bemused expression. In nineteen years, he hadn't changed a bit.

Martin wondered if he was imagining the whole thing.

"You took Andrew."

"I took him?" His voice was smooth, almost guileless. "That's not the way I remember it. The way I recall, you were all too eager to give him away."

Martin had thought about that night, their conversation in the park, too often to be able to deny what he was saying. "But you said, you said three days."

The man nodded. "Yes I did."

"It's been nineteen years," he almost shouted. He had missed another anniversary, but he never lost track of the time.

"Here," the man said flatly.

"What?" At first Martin thought it was the drugs, that he had lost track of the conversation.

"It's been nineteen years *here*," the man said, as if explaining something to an idiot. "But by my watch," he looked at his wrist. "It's only been . . . what? Two and a half days? A little more?"

"Relativity," Martin muttered, surrendering to the suspicion that he was hallucinating the entire conversation. There was no way the man in black could be here—it had to be a dream.

"Something like that. I think I read somewhere that on Venus, a day is something like six thousand earth hours long. Two hundred and forty three earth days for one day on Venus. Makes you think, doesn't it?"

Martin wasn't feeling capable of thought.

"And if your brother was in a place where a single day took seven years to pass, well, he'd be arriving home in just a few hours." He looked at Martin meaningfully. "That's a bit less than two years from now."

Martin groaned, struggling to cling to the threads of the conversation.

"Three days. Just like we agreed."

He tried to sit up. And failed.

The man stood up next to the bed and looked down at Martin.

"Of course, things aren't looking too good for you right now, are they? You keep this up, you're gonna be the one not to make it the three days."

Martin couldn't help but think of Rudy Cezzoni, the look on his face, the shouted promise that he was going to finish the job. No, things weren't looking too good for him right now.

As if reading his mind, the man said, "If you're worrying about that fellow who attacked you, who put that slice in your back, don't. He won't be troubling you again."

For a moment, Martin's vision of the man seemed to waver and shift. His black coat became, for an instant, a guard's uniform. His hair was cut short, regulation-length, and he was covered in blood, soaked in it, his hand stained red, his face sprayed.

Then Martin blinked and everything was normal again, the man looking down at him, almost comfortingly.

But when he laid his hand on Martin's arm, Martin felt himself pull back from the warmth.

"I'm worried about you," the man said, not noticing. "Look at you. You spend your days lying around, intoxicated by whatever means you can find, dying by inches. It's pathetic, really."

Martin was too stunned by the man's knowledge, the accuracy of his description, to take offence.

"If things don't change, I don't think you'll make it."

"Make what?" he asked, still trying to follow along.

"The day your brother will come home," he said. "What did you think we'd been talking about?"

"Andrew?" He could feel himself starting to lose the fight against the morphine.

"If you don't change, you'll either be dead or you'll be in here. Amounts to the same thing."

The warm fog of the drug started to lay heavily upon him. "Andrew?"

"I've stayed too long," the man said. "You need your rest."

"But . . ."

"Remember what I said, Martin. I always keep my word. Three days. Midnight on the third day."

"Andrew . . ."

But the man had already stepped away. "I'll see you soon, Martin. Stay well."

Without any fanfare, the man seemed to turn to one side and to take a step around a corner in the air that Martin couldn't see. He disappeared, as if he had never been there.

Martin slipped back into sleep almost instantly, falling back into the warm softness of the morphine.

His last thoughts were the words "three days, seven years."

Martin watched Tommy leave the coffee shop, turn around the corner and walk away, Marco falling into step behind him. He never glanced back at the table where Martin was sitting, and gave no hint of even recognizing him.

Marco looked back at him, though. A quick glance before walking away that Martin wouldn't have caught if he hadn't been watching for it.

He sighed, looked down at the untouched coffee cup in front of him. He wasn't convinced by Tommy's assessment of the kid's loyalty. He wasn't comforted.

Blood ties.

Ah well. After tonight, it probably wouldn't matter.

He waited several minutes, smoking another cigarette, before he went inside. Getting the key from the barista, he let himself into the men's room.

It only took him a few seconds—the room was pretty bare, without a lot of practical hiding places.

The gun was in the first place he looked, tucked into the trash can between the liner and the metal body of the can itself.

Lifting it with an exaggerated care, he hefted the gun in his hand. It was a good weight—solid, but not too heavy. It was matte black, and seemed to swallow the light it touched.

He looked down the short barrel, turned it in his hand, feeling for its balance.

It would do.

He was putting the garbage can back together when he saw that

Tommy had left him another gift, a plastic zip-top bag crammed deep in the container.

The bag was surprisingly heavy: a double handful of pills in a rainbow of colours. A chunk of hash and a big, crystally bud. A couple of tinfoil twists. A smaller bag of white powder. A small vial of rock.

Martin smiled at the thought of his friend carefully putting the bag together for him, tucking it lovingly into the garbage bin alongside the gun. "Just in case you change your mind," he imagined Tommy saying.

The thought warmed him, and he shifted the bag into the inside pocket of his jacket. The he slipped the gun into the waistband of his pants, looking at himself critically in the mirror to be sure that the bulge wasn't too obvious with his jacket done up a bit. He had to be careful: it wouldn't do to get picked up by the cops for packing a gun. Not tonight. Not yet.

He turned to one side, then the other, looking at himself. It seemed fine—a slight bulge, but nothing obvious.

He washed his hands in the sink, and ran his wet fingers through his short hair, meeting his own eyes in the mirror.

Tonight. Now.

The van bounced with every bump, lurching and rattling. Martin tried to ignore it as best he could. The vehicles from Corrections weren't built for comfort; hopefully, this would be the last one he would be riding in.

"It must have been hard for you."

Martin glanced up at the van's driver through the grated metal barrier. He assumed the guard was talking on a cell phone or on the radio until he saw the man's eyes looking back at him in the rear-view mirror.

It was just the two of them in the van, but Martin still wasn't convinced that the guard was talking to him. "What?"

"You're Martin Corbett, right?"

Martin nodded, surprised.

"I remember what happened. With your brother."

Martin tried not to sigh. "Yeah."

"That must have been hard for you," the guard said. He was an older man, probably close to sixty, with longish silver hair and a full beard. He had the softness that some of the guards got, a puffiness that did little to hide the strength underneath. "Having to go through all that."

Martin nodded, almost speechless. It had been years since someone had even hinted at what it had been like for him. If they remembered his brother at all, it was usually a matter of *I wonder whatever happened. . . . Poor kid.*

"It was. Hard, I mean."

The guard nodded. "I remember watching the news when it happened, seeing them talking to you. You were so young, and I knew—I said to my wife—that kid's carrying an awful lot of this. Shouldn't have to. Not when you're so young."

Martin couldn't think of anything to say. "So how did you know my name?"

"I've got your file," he said, gesturing at the papers on the seat next to him. "On my coffee break I read through your sheet, then I looked at the name and the penny dropped. It explained a lot, when I remembered seeing you before."

"Like what? What did it explain?" Genuinely curious.

"Like how you managed to make such a shit-heap of your life in such a short time." The guard glanced back at him, gauging his reaction. "I mean, I've driven guys twice your age that don't have sheets half as long as yours. Assault. Assault with intent. Possession with intent. Possession of a weapon. Armed robbery. . . . And you're what? Thirty?"

"Thirty-three."

"Right. Well, knowing where you came from, what all you went through, that explains a lot. Doesn't excuse anything, though."

"No." Martin shook his head. "No, it doesn't."

"But I look at you—" He glanced again in the rear-view mirror. "I drive a lot of guys to a lot of hearings. A lot. Parole hearings, mostly. And most of 'em, you can just tell their changes are an hour old and a hair deep. They think that if they get new haircuts, and spend a couple of minutes yes-sirring and no-sirring and wouldn't-hurt-a-fly-sirring, the judge is just gonna let them out. It works a lot of the time, too. But I look at you, and I don't see that. You look like maybe you've really changed."

Martin didn't say anything, didn't move to agree or disagree.

"You've been working in the library."

He nodded. "A little more than a year now."

"You like that?"

"It makes the time pass," he answered. It had also allowed him to spend a lot of time on his own with the books, trying to figure out what the man in black had been talking about, trying to figure out how three days could be twenty-one years.

He thought he understood now. He thought he knew where Andrew had been all this time, and where he would be coming back. Assuming the man in black hadn't been lying to him, jerking him around. His kind were known for doing that: lying, or playing games with words and their meanings.

Three days. Seven years.

"I bet it does. Most of the guys I drive, they take on a job like that a month or two before their hearing, really try to look like they've cleaned up their act. It's different for you, though, isn't it?"

Martin nodded. "I like to think so."

They spent most of the rest of the drive in silence, with Martin thinking ahead to the hearing that was waiting for him. He needed to get it exactly right. He needed to be out. There were no second chances. If his petition for parole failed, he'd be inside on the anniversary of Andrew's disappearance.

He wouldn't be there when he brother came back.

He wouldn't be there to put a bullet in the man who had stolen his brother.

❧

The park was dark, its shadows broken only occasionally by bright pools from the tall floodlights.

Martin kept to the dark and the shadows. It wasn't cold, but he pulled his jacket tightly around himself, shivering a little. It all came down to this: all the years of absence, all the years of pain, and it all came down to tonight.

He was grateful for the gun, tucked into the waistband of his jeans.

He had no reason to believe Jack when he said that Andrew would be coming back. He had no reason, he knew, to believe that the man was anything other than a figment of his imagination. But for some reason he trusted him. He would be here. Martin was sure of it.

And soon, he thought, glancing at his watch. It was almost twelve. Almost the end of twenty one years. Almost the end—somewhere else—of three days.

He pressed himself into the shadow along the outside wall of the right-field dug-out as a small group of kids passed. Two girls and two boys, laughing uproariously, shouting at each other, pushing and jostling and passing a joint from hand to hand to hand. They passed so closely he could have reached out and touched any of them. He smiled at the thought of how freaked out they would have been, and once they were gone he allowed himself to relax.

He looked at his watch again. Almost.

He almost heard them in time. There was a noise—the sound of a breath? The soft crunch of gravel underfoot?—and he started to turned, but it was too late.

The first punch caught him in mid-turn, crunching against the left side of his jaw near his ear. A bright flash of pain and he reeled, spinning toward another punch that broke his nose, that cracked two of his front teeth.

He tried to put his hands up, tried to turn himself out of the way, but there were too many of them. No matter how he turned he was met by punches, blows raining in on him, forcing him to his knees.

He could taste his own blood as they started to kick him, heavy boots cracking his ribs, driving the breath from him. When a steel toe connected with his kidney, he thought he was going to pass out. The world spun away from him, shifting in and out of focus, fading to dark.

Hands at his shoulders. Pulling him up. Pressing him against the wall of the dugout. A fist driven into his stomach, but he couldn't fall.

"You think you're so fucking cool," the voice hissed into his ear, stinking of garlic. Martin tried to see, but he was too close, and it was too dark.

"You waltz back into town all fuckin' big man and shit, but you ain't nothin'."

The voice stepped back, into the light. Marco. The light shone off the smoothness of his head, off the edge of the knife he held up in front of Martin's eyes.

"You're not so fucking tough, are you? Not so tough now." The kid sneered, and turned the knife to catch the light. "You scared? You gonna cry now?"

Martin hadn't cried in more than twenty years—he wouldn't give the kid the satisfaction. Instead he tried to raise his hand, tried to meet his eye.

"I didn't—" Every word was an agony, every breath sending waves of pain through him. "I didn't kill your brother," he said.

But it didn't matter.

Marco buried the knife in Martin's chest, just below the ribs on his right side.

Martin didn't feel the blade go in: there was a moment between the impact, which felt like a punch, and the pain, a moment when he felt like maybe he was going to be okay, that maybe Marco had decided to teach him a lesson, rather than to kill him.

That hope vanished with a wave of pain that forced his head back, that forced a scream from him.

Marco leaned in close, the smell of him in the space between them, and met Martin's eyes. "This is for my brother," he said slowly, as he twisted the knife.

The darkness rose up mercifully, and swallowed him.

❧

He wasn't aware of opening his eyes: one moment there was darkness and the next there was light. He was lying on the ground, the world heaving and buckling under him, within him. It almost felt like a bad trip, and he thought that if he just managed to ride this out. . . .

But he knew there was no riding this out. He could feel himself getting weaker, his life draining away through the hole in his chest. His vision swam. The gravel path under him was a slurry of blood and dirt.

He could barely move. When he tried to turn, his body screamed out in pain, and the darkness threatened to take him again. He could barely breathe, and he coughed blood in mouthfuls onto the ground. He pushed his hand into his jacket, pressed it against the wound in his chest. His shirt was wet and hot with his own blood, and the opening seemed to suck at his hand.

It was no good. It was all too much. There was no way he was going to make it.

As the darkness was about to take him, the park seemed to fill with light. Not anything electrical—not a floodlight. Not a police car. This was a warm golden light, a light that felt of summer evenings, a light that felt of ease, of long mornings in bed, of walks along the rocky beach with a girl. Of a life he had never known.

Andrew . . .

He opened his eyes, watched the light move along the dugout walls.

It took him almost all of his strength to turn over, to face the source of the light.

It seemed to be a rectangle, a door, hanging in the air in the darkness. The light spilled from it in what seemed to be waves, a slow undulation of warmth that seemed to beckon him, to call him toward it.

Grinding his teeth together, he pulled himself to his knees, pressing his left hand against the hole in his chest. Every motion caused blood to gush from it, and his body was slick.

Looking into the light, he pushed himself slowly, unsteadily, to his feet. Narrowing his eyes, he thought he could see motion in the light, movement like shifting shadows. People. He could hear music. Voices.

He took a step forward, almost falling as the world lurched away from him.

His right hand fell to the butt of the gun, and he pulled it from his pants. He could barely lift it, and the pistol hung at his waist.

The light seemed to brighten, the golden warmth brighter than anything he had ever seen, but not blinding. He could feel the heat against his face, the warmth enveloping him, holding him tight, the voices seeming to whisper to him.

He took another step forward.

He had been waiting for this moment for his entire life. He had chased and sought the light through every moment, waiting to taste that ease, that warmth, that comfort. . . .

The gun fell to the ground as he took another step.

The shadows moved within the light, shifted and swam, dissolved and coalesced. Figures. People. He thought he could see dark figures moving toward him, shades against the bright warmth, shades gaining form as they moved toward him, as he moved toward them. A tall, dark shape. A smaller one. A man. A boy.

A boy . . .

Martin choked back a sob, couldn't bring his mouth to form words. He took another halting step forward. Another. He couldn't hold up his arm anymore, and it fell to his side. His blood flowed freely, spilling onto the ground as he took another step.

And another.

Toward the light.

THE SMALL RAIN DOWN

The rain came as I pulled into my parents' driveway. It had been threatening since I crossed the bridge, the air heavy and wet on my face when I stopped at the railroad tracks, stinging slightly as I drove.

I parked the car beside the house and scrambled out to put up the top. The asphalt was slippery, plastered with the first of the fallen leaves.

The sound of laughter from the shadow under the chestnut tree made me look up. Isabel was leaning against her car in the near-darkness, arms folded across her chest, watching me.

I smiled, and finished putting up the top with a methodical nonchalance before walking over to her.

"Afraid you're gonna melt?" she asked, biting her lip.

"You're the one hiding under the tree."

"I wanted to surprise you."

"You did."

I wasn't sure if I should kiss her or give her a noncommittal, keep-it-brief, keep-it-safe hug. How do you say hello to someone you haven't seen in twenty years, someone who you once shared everything with?

She took care of my uncertainty by leaning forward and kissing me, her lips lingering a moment too long on mine. She pulled away but stayed close, leaning her forehead against my chest just below the hollow of my throat. Her hand came up to toy with the hair at the back of my head.

"Too late putting the top up," she said, showing me the wet on her hand from my hair. "You're already starting to melt."

"I told you before," I said, closing my eyes a little at her touch. "I'm not that sweet."

"I haven't heard you say that in—"

"Twenty years," I finished for her. "I haven't gotten any sweeter."

She stepped away from me, and I immediately began to miss the warmth of her, the smell of her hair, her perfume.

"No, I bet you haven't." She made it almost sound like a joke, but she had folded her arms across her chest again.

I took a step back, kicked at a chestnut husk. "So how did you know I'd be here?"

"I knew you'd come back for the funeral."

"Yeah."

The rain picked up, and echoed off the canopy of yellow leaves. I glanced back at my car, triple-checking that the windows were closed.

"But how did you know when? Did you just guess, or . . ."

She shrugged. She hadn't changed. "I was fine waiting."

"You could have gone into the house. I'm sure Mom and Dad . . ." I stopped myself.

"I was fine in the car. I turned the heater up, put on some music."

She smiled a teasing smile, and it took me a moment to put it together. "Holy shit," I said, leaning over to look at the car more closely. "Is this the same piece of shit car—?"

She nodded, her smile broadening. "The one and only."

I tapped at the rust patch by the front wheel-well with the toe of my shoe. Flakes fell to the driveway. "Unbelievable," I muttered. "This car was a junker back when. . . ."

"Yeah."

"Did you ever get the steering fixed?"

She shrugged again. "It does the job."

"Unbelievable," I repeated. "We sure had some good times in this car."

When I looked up, she was watching me. Our eyes met. "Yeah."

"I remember driving up to the lake in the middle of the night, windows down, listening to that REM tape."

"Yeah."

I'd said all that I really felt comfortable saying. More than.

"Yeah," I agreed, with myself.

The chestnut hit the roof in an explosion of spiny shell segments.

"Shit!" she shouted, jumping away from the car.

I laughed. "That's why we don't park under the tree in the fall. I figured you would have remembered that."

"Apparently not."

A stronger wind caught under the leaves, and the canopy shifted overhead. More chestnuts fell around us, and the rain blew in, cold and hard.

"Come on," I said. "Let's go inside."

We hurried across the driveway and up the walk to the back door. It was only when I bent to pick up the flowerpot where Mom had always hidden the spare key that I realized we were holding hands. It felt entirely natural. I didn't know which one of us had reached out first.

I had to let go to unlock the door. She was looking at the ground when I turned to her.

"Some things never change," I said, as I turned the key in the lock, only realizing what I had said when I put it back into the flowerpot.

She still wasn't looking at me.

"Well," I said as I opened the back door. "Can I take your coat?"

Inside, the house was cool and dim, with the silence and stillness that only an empty house can possess. I kicked my shoes onto the mat instinctively, the way I always had. Catching myself, I bent over and placed them neatly together, toes against the wall.

Isabel was watching me, half-smiling. "Danny the champion of the world, all growed up."

She stepped out of her shoes as I tried to figure out how I should take her comment.

She hung her jacket on the hook behind the door and ran her fingers over her hair, flicking the water away.

I realized, watching her, that I had absolutely no idea what to say to her next. It seemed like there should be so much, so many words, but I couldn't think of anything.

"Can I get you a drink?"

She smiled.

In the kitchen, I opened the cupboard door and looked at the bottles within. It was dim in the room, but the glass caught the light.

"Twenty years later and I'm still pilfering my parents' liquor. What'll you have?"

She looked over my shoulder. "Rum and Coke sounds good."

"Jesus," I muttered, my mouth curling as I remembered the cloying taste. "How can you drink that?" I asked as I put the rum bottle on the counter.

She shrugged. "It reminds me of high school."

"Yeah, that's the problem," I said, putting a bottle of gin beside the rum, sliding the cupboard door shut.

"Why is rum and Coke a problem?"

"Rum and Coke," I answered from the fridge, looking for mix. "Is what teenage girls drink when they know they should be drinking but they don't really want to. All in the name of getting to the stuff they know they shouldn't be doing, but really want to."

"I seem to recall that working out pretty well for you."

I smiled. "A time or two."

"Hence my fond memories of rum and Coke."

"The good old days," I said. I handed her glass to her.

"To the good old days," she said, tilting her glass toward me.

We clinked the rims, and drank.

There was a long moment of silence.

"This isn't nearly as strong as you used to make them," she said, studying her glass.

"I'm not trying to get into your pants." I smiled broadly.

She seemed a bit surprised, and took another drink. "Hmm."

She turned to face the room, and I followed her gaze: the dining room table with its runner and wooden bowl of nuts. The photographs on the walls. The view through the trees to the road beyond.

"This feels awfully familiar," she said.

"Yeah."

"You and me in this house, your parents gone. . . ."

"Yeah."

"For a weekend or a week or a whole month."

"Yeah."

"I seem to recall that working out pretty well for you, too."

The year that Isabel and I were seeing each other, the year we were fifteen and sixteen, my parents were away a lot. Contracts in Vancouver and Toronto, holidays to the Bahamas and Europe. A cruise vacation up the Yangtze River that kept them away for five weeks. Isabel and I spent practically every waking moment together, most of them alone in this house. We'd watch movies and work on our homework, take baths together, smoking dope in the tub, reading poetry. We spent whole days naked, cooking soup, making love in front of the fire—

"Should we light a fire?" she asked.

It was like she had been reading my mind, but of course she'd be having the same memories.

"Sure," I said, following her into the living room.

"Well," she said, stopping in front of the fireplace and leaning over. "Do you want to do the honours?"

True to form, my father had left a fire laid in the hearth. Fumbling with the flue and the vents, I struck one of the long matches and touched it to the crumpled newspaper. The flames raced along the edge of the paper, the kindling caught and then there was a fire, better than I could have built.

"That's nice," she said, sinking into one of the chairs. "I would have thought that your parents would have upgraded to natural gas, though."

I shrugged and settled myself across from her. The flames crackled loudly. "I . . . I wouldn't really know."

She nodded, took a sip from her drink. "I guess," she said. "What happened there? With your folks I mean? With you just . . ."

"Leaving?" I asked.

"I was going to say 'disappeared,'" she said. "You were just gone. I mean, you let everyone know where you were going, but you never. . . . This is your first trip back."

"Yeah."

"In twenty years."

"And not the best of circumstances," I said, thinking ahead to the funeral the next afternoon.

"No, not the best," she agreed. "So what happened, back then, back when you left?"

"It's not like there's any big secret or anything," I said, taking a swallow of my drink. The gin and tonic had been a mistake. It made me think of a hot summer day in New York, a patio in the Village or a rooftop party, and I wished I had chosen something else, something more appropriate. Next time. Maybe rye next time. Or scotch. Something dark, smoky, tasting of the fall.

"Danny Rush, always rushing off," she teased me, the way she used to.

I smiled. "I didn't have a big fight with my parents or anything. I just—it was time. I had to go. I had to start, had to start my life, you know? It was what we had always talked about, getting out. Getting free. I mean, Henderson, it's a good place to come from—"

"People build good lives here, Danny," she said, and I thought I heard defensiveness in her voice.

"Oh, I know. And that's why I had to go. Right then. Why I had to go and keep going. It would have been so easy, so tempting, to just build a life here. Get a job, get married, have kids. Too easy."

"So you went to Paris." She set her empty glass on the coffee table.

"Do you want—" I gestured at the glass.

She shook her head. "I want to hear about Paris."

"Well, I thought I should make some use of my hard-won grade twelve French before it disappeared entirely. Turns out you don't need a lot of French to live in Paris." I drained my glass and set it on the table across from hers.

"Did you stay there, or . . . ?"

"Not then, no. No, I spent, God, I don't even remember how long, just travelling around. Europe, North Africa. I spent a winter in Greece tending bar, practically living on the beach. I saw the pyramids, and the Hagia Sophia. I ran with the bulls in Pamplona, crossed the Sahara, smoked opium with tribesmen in Morocco."

"Everything you dreamed of in high school," she said. Her eyes were wide, but she didn't seem too surprised. I assumed she'd already heard most of the stories. Or read about them.

"And more," I said. "After that, I went back to Paris. I had a little money, but all I could afford was this dive, five floors up. I spent the winter writing in cafes, in these French school notebooks, these cahiers, with a secondhand fountain pen—"

"How very Hemingway of you," she said drily.

I smiled, knowing how I sounded. "Very *Moveable Feast*, yeah."

She folded her legs under herself, leaning back in the chair. "And then?"

"And then . . ." I sighed. "And then I published a book. And another. I got a nicer apartment, but I decided to move to New York."

"And you're still there."

I nodded. "Yeah, I've got a place in the Village. I'm still writing, but it's more movies now than books. I've got a place in San Francisco where I spend most of my time. Close enough to be close enough to L.A., but not so close I have to be part of it. That's where I was when I heard. . . ."

"And you drove up."

"Yeah. I like to drive. Especially the 1 and the 101 up the coast through California and Oregon. Good for the soul."

She nodded as if she understood. "And you never came back. You never hopped in your car and just decided, 'Hey, I'm gonna pay the old hometown a visit.'"

"I thought about it. Especially being so close. But all this—" I gestured around the room, the house, the town "—it's best in the past for me. A memory. It's a good place to come from—"

The burnt, reduced embers of a log fell against the fireplace grate and I stood up to throw another log on the dying flames.

"Leave it," she said, almost in a whisper.

"What?" I asked, turning to her.

She unfolded herself from the chair. "Leave the fire. Let's go for a drive."

{

Neither of us said much as we drove around the valley. I had the wheel, turning where she asked me to turn, slowing down when she told me to slow down.

She had grabbed a tape from her car and popped it into the stereo as I pulled us out of the driveway. The familiar, folksy guitars brought a smile to my face.

"REM?"

"Hey, if you're gonna take a journey through the past, you might as well do it right."

We did it right that afternoon. We drove miles down those country roads, the yellowing corn growing right to the edge of the asphalt in places. I kept the top up against the intermittent rain that spattered the windshield, but we both had our windows down. The air smelled of autumn, of drying leaves and rain, smoke from backyard fires and an undertone of decay, of fields plowed under and waiting for the spring.

"You know what I remember?" she said as we rolled along a familiar stretch of road. "I remember us frantically getting dressed and getting on our bikes to race my curfew home. Every night. You used to kiss me goodnight at the top of the driveway so my dad wouldn't see."

I smiled at the memory. "Did you know I used to stop in town on the way home? I'd go to the pizza place, have a slice, find someone to play a game of chess."

She shook her head. "I didn't know. Why'd you do that?"

"I didn't want to go home alone."

She didn't say anything for a long moment, and I looked out the window at the cornfields.

"It got better, though, once you got your driver's licence, and that piece of shit car," I said at length, trying to put the conversation back on track. "At least then we weren't hurtling through the night on our ten speeds."

"And you always came with me, then walked all the way home." Her voice was warm at the thought.

"Yeah. I wanted—" I tightened my hands around the wheel "—I wanted to spend as much time with you as I could. I didn't want the days to end. Not like that. I wanted. . . . You know what I always dreamed of? I dreamed of spending the night with you. Waking up in the morning and having you there with me. We never had that."

"I thought we would," she said. "I thought we'd have a lifetime of nights together."

I couldn't say anything to that.

With the sun on the horizon, I pulled up to the crossroads where the highway met the lake road.

"Left," she said.

"Up to the lake?" I asked, flipping the turn indicator.

"Unless you've got other plans."

I eased into the turn.

As the sky darkened, we took a walk along the beach. A cold wind had blown up off the water, and I gave her a coat out of my trunk.

The lights of the hotels and restaurants danced along the water, and voices and music spilled along the wind from the Bird of Paradise. The moon, almost full, appeared and disappeared as clouds drifted by.

I took her hand. It felt like the most natural thing in the world.

"Are you happy?" she asked, not looking at me.

I squeezed her hand gently. "I am."

"No." She shook her head. "Not now. When you're at home, in New York or San Francisco. Are you happy? Is there someone there, worrying about you?"

I shrugged. "Not anyone permanent," I said, thinking about the last few women I had dated. "I see. . . . I date. Some. I work. Mostly it's work."

"Are you happy?"

I thought for a moment.

"Never mind," she said. "If you have to think about it that long, it's probably not something you want to be thinking about."

I didn't even try to argue.

"This must seem pretty boring to you," she said after a while. "Compared to Paris and Morocco and New York and all those other places I've never been."

"Right now," I said, meeting her eyes, "there's no place in the world I'd rather be."

She smiled, and her hand tightened around mine. A gust swept across us, and she shivered.

"You're cold."

"I'm fine."

"We should go back."

"No, I—I'd like to keep going, just a little longer."

"Here," I said, drawing her close and encircling her with my arm. "Is that better?"

"Mmhmm," she said, snuggling herself tightly against me.

We walked like that, nestled into one another, until the rain came, black sheets of icy spray thundering off the sand and the water. We ran back to the car, laughing and shivering, soaked almost to the skin.

{

"This is getting to be a habit," she laughed as I fumbled with the key to the back door. "Coming back here all wet."

"We'll have you fixed up in no time," I said as the door opened and we scurried in. "I'll get you a robe or something to put on while your clothes are in the dryer." I kicked off my shoes and my socks squelched against the floor.

"No, that's okay," she said. "They'll dry quick enough."

My jacket landed with a wet thud.

"That's crazy talk," I said. She was pale, her lips only slightly pink against the white of her face, her jaw trembling. "You're freezing. Your teeth are chattering. Listen, go in and have a hot shower. Leave your clothes outside the door and I'll bring you something warm to put on."

She pulled her jacket off and dropped it on the floor beside my own. "I'm really okay." Her shirt was soaked, and plastered to her skin.

"Well I'm not," I said. "I'm gonna have a quick heat-up in the upstairs shower while you do the same down here."

She started to speak, but I stopped her. "I'm not going to take no for an answer. Take your time. I'll leave a robe hanging on the doorknob."

She smiled shyly, paused for a moment, then turned away. I waited until I heard the bathroom door close before I allowed myself the full body shiver I had been holding back. "Jesus," I muttered. I took the stairs two at a time, clutching my arms across my chest, so cold I thought my own teeth might start chattering.

I turned on the heat lamp in my parents' en suite and pulled off my clothes as quickly as I could, dropping my socks and pants and underwear in a heap on the floor. My shirt clung cold and wet to my face as I pulled it over my head.

When I had struggled free, Isabel was standing in the doorway.

My first impulse was to cover myself, but I didn't. I looked at her, met her eye.

"I thought—" she started, looking at me.

"Okay," I said. "You should—you're gonna catch your death."

She nodded and stepped forward, closing the door gently behind herself. Without looking away, she reached down and unbuttoned her pants.

I could feel the heat from the ceiling lamp against my naked shoulders, and I imagined steam rising from me.

She shucked off her pants, and in almost the same motion pulled off her shirt.

"I thought," she said, reaching behind herself for her bra. "I thought I'd stay. Tonight. With you. If that's—"

The bra fell noiselessly to the floor, and she stepped gingerly out of her underpants.

I thought of how shy she had been the first few times we had made love, insisting that I turn out the lights, blow out the candles. I had memorized her body, every curve and sway, long before I ever saw it.

I thought maybe it was just the passage of time which had changed her, had given her strength, but then I remembered that summer day, a few months after we had been making love, the hike that had taken us into the hills on the hottest day of the year.

We had stopped at the side of a creek, and I sat on a rock at the water's edge, kicking off my boots and dangling my feet in the glacial water.

When I looked up at her, she was naked, her pale skin almost incandescent in the afternoon sun. She had smiled, I guess at my expression.

"This is me," she had said, as if bestowing me with a great secret.

"Thank you," I had said, knowing without understanding that this was the right thing to say.

Standing in my parents' bathroom, more than two decades later, I wanted to thank her again. I wanted to thank her for being brave enough to cross that final distance between us, that infinitesimally small, infinitely large gap that had been there since I had pulled into the yard and found her there waiting. I don't know that I would have had the courage.

"Is that all right?" she asked. "If I stay?"

I nodded. "I would like that. I would like that very much."

We stayed in the shower until the water ran out, then we lingered under the heat lamp, drying each other with my mother's fluffy white towels until our skin shone.

{

We slept, as we always had, in my mother and father's bed. I didn't bother checking my old room. I knew that whether I found my old twin, intact after all these years, or a new guest room, it wouldn't measure up to the room that we knew so well.

I woke to the sound of rain against the roof, hard and relentless. The room was dark, save for the dim slice of light from under the bathroom door.

"I like the sound of the rain," she whispered. I could feel her words against my chest. Her voice was soft and distant, sleep-drugged and languorous.

We just lay there for a long while, listening to the sound of the rain, the sound of one another's breathing.

"You used to know a poem," she said. "About the rain. You used to say it when we were lying together like this. Something about the wind and the rain."

I didn't even have to think about it. "'Oh western wind, when wilt thou blow,'" I started. "'That the small rain down can rain? Christ, that my love were in my arms, and I in my bed again. . . .'"

"That's the one," she said, in a voice that sounded like she was lost somewhere in a dream. "Say it again."

As I repeated the words, I could feel the heaviness of sleep upon her, heard her breathing slow. My love in my arms, and I in my bed again.

We curled together in the middle of the bed, our bodies so twisted into one another that it was impossible to tell where one of us began and the other ended.

In that way, we slept the night together for the first time.

{

When I woke up, the room was light, but I had no idea where I was, no memory of how I had come to be there. I scrambled for a moment, pulling the covers tightly around me, until I saw Isabel and remembered. She had raised herself up on one elbow and was smiling at me, an odd, knowing smile.

"Izzy," I said, as if I hadn't seen her for years. "You're . . ."

"I'm here, Daniel," she said. "Right where you left me."

I reached out, touched the side of her face, the warmth of her cheek. "You're here," I said, feeling stupid.

She leaned over and kissed me, her lips lingering against mine. "I'm here," she breathed.

I slumped back against the bed, muscles relaxing that I wasn't even aware that I had tensed.

"Are you all right?" she asked.

"I had. . . . I had a dream," I confessed, feeling even more stupid.

"A nightmare?"

"Yes. No. I don't know. I've had it, the same dream, the last few nights. Ever since I heard the news and started back here."

"Do you want to talk about it?"

What I wanted, more than anything, was to kiss the hollow of her throat.

"It's . . . I'm sure it's just coming back here, all the memories, all the thoughts that's bringing up. . . ." I traced my fingers along her clavicle, across the warmth of her throat, feeling the warm pulse of her there.

"It's about all this," I said, trying to find a way to begin. "It's about . . . Henderson. And me. What my life would have been like if I had never left."

"That must have been a nightmare for you," she said. "And what would that have been like?"

"I . . . Some of it's so vivid. I can see myself running the newspaper, joking around with the guys who run the press. Frank and Jim." I shook my head, finding it hard to believe that I could actually remember the names of people in a dream.

"I can see myself having dinner with my parents, every Sunday night. My parents and . . . my wife," I said carefully, watching her to see how she would respond. "I've got a wife. And two little kids. Two boys. Michael and Stephen."

"That sounds nice," she said, curling in closer to me.

"It is. I mean, I think it is. It's strange—it was one of those dreams where I'm inside myself, but I'm watching myself from outside at the same time. So I don't know. I think I'm happy, but I'm not really experiencing it directly. Does that make any sense?"

"As much as dreams ever do," she said. "And where am I in this path not taken? Am I the doting wife, or have I been demoted to that girl you used to know?"

She sounded so happy, so casual and jokey, that I almost couldn't bear to tell her.

"You're not," I started. "See that's, that's the thing. You . . . you're not around. Right at the beginning, right at the start of the dream, you. . . ." I tightened my arm around her. "You die."

"What?" The word bubbled out of her like a laugh, and her face broke into a broad smile. "I die?"

I nodded slowly.

"So let me get this straight—you've managed to write me out of this fantasy version of your life as well? Jesus, Danny, a girl could get a complex."

She was joking, but I was still feeling the strange aftereffects of the dream, unable to so quickly put aside what I had seen, what I had felt.

"It's not like that," I tried to explain.

"I know," she said. "I was just. . . ."

"It was terrible," I said. "You were driving, and I was watching, and you . . . you took a corner wrong and you went into this ditch, full of water. You drowned, right there in front of me, and there was nothing I could do. . . ."

"Shh," she said, gently touching my face. "It's all right. I'm right here."

"I know." I pulled her closer to me, close enough I could smell her hair, kiss her on the forehead. "I know you are."

She kissed me at the corner of my mouth.

"It's weird. You were so young. We both were. And you died, and that's . . . it was like that changed everything. After that, it's like I didn't have the courage to leave. I just . . ." I couldn't even put a sentence together, couldn't concentrate on anything other than the gentle touch of her fingertips on my face.

"Then it's a good thing for you that I'm still here." I could hear the smile in her voice, but my eyes had slipped shut, and I was drifting away.

{

"Were you happy?" she asked from the doorway. We had kept the curtains closed and, coming back from the bathroom, the pale length of her seemed to glow in the half-light.

"What, just now?"

She climbed back into the bed, drawing the covers up around the two of us. "No," she said. "I got the impression you were pretty happy just then. No, in your dream: were you happy?"

I pulled her to me, almost atop me, blanketed by her warmth. "I lost you," I whispered. "Again."

"Aside from that," she said. "It didn't sound like it was a bad life."

I brushed her hair back from her face. "No. No, it wasn't, I guess. I had a family, a job, people I knew, people who knew me. It would have been a fine life. For someone else."

"A lot of people are happy with lives like that."

"It wasn't mine, though. Even in the dream, I could feel like there were things I should have been doing, different choices I should have made."

"Everybody has regrets."

"I know. I have a few of my own." I looked at her meaningfully.

She smiled. "You learn to live with them. You build the best life you can. You die happy."

The word was a potent reminder, and we both looked at the clock.

"We should start getting ready," she sighed.

"Yeah." The thin edge of my agreement slid into me like a blade. I didn't want to leave this bed, this room, this moment.

Isabel didn't seem to want to move, either.

"Let's throw some clothes on. I'll run you into your place so you can pick up some proper attire—" I stretched out the words "—and we can get ready together here."

She shook her head. "No need."

"What?"

She smiled, a little shyly, and her cheeks coloured. "I don't need to go home. I've got a dress and some stuff in the car."

My smile broadened as I reckoned with the implications of her words.

"I was hoping you would ask me to stay," she explained, still blushing. "That was one of my regrets, too, that we had never spent a night together. That I had never woke up a morning in your arms. That I had never watched you dream."

Her words warmed me, and I felt even less like rising from the bed. "You watched me? When I was having that dream?"

She nodded. "You were smiling."

⁂

After showering, we dressed side by side in my parents' bedroom, in front of the broad mirror fronting their closets. I had a charcoal suit, with a plain white shirt and a dark tie. She wore a simple black dress, and a silver chain around her neck.

"I'm sorry," I said quietly to her reflection as I tied my tie.

"For what?" Carefully putting in an earring.

"For leaving like that. Without you."

"That was a long time ago."

I shrugged.

"It would have changed everything."

"Still, I'm sorry. I think I would have liked to see what a life with you would have been like."

"I might not even have gone," she said, her reflection smiling mischievously.

"Really?"

She shrugged. "I don't know. I tend to be pretty capricious. I was even worse back then."

I smiled, then looked down at the floor. "It's not too late," I almost whispered, half-hoping that she wouldn't hear. I felt ridiculous, putting so much weight on a single night. But it wasn't just a single night, was it?

I felt her hand on my arm, and when I looked up, her reflection was staring at me. "Yes," she whispered. "Yes it is. Too late. You can't go back."

"This isn't—this wouldn't be going back. This would be going forward. . . ."

Her reflection shook her head. "You know that's not true. We've made our choices, both of us. They can't be unmade. We can't uncreate the people we've become."

I started to argue with her, but I couldn't. I knew what she was saying to be true.

"We had our night, Daniel. And that's something I'll never forget. But it doesn't change anything."

I thought she was wrong about that, but I couldn't be sure.

{

We drove in silence to the cemetery. The road was another of those long country roads, straight, with cornfields on both sides, yellow and dry. It was still grey and cloudy, but the rain had stopped, and I took the top down. As we drove, the wind played with our hair.

She smiled, but kept her eyes fixed on the road ahead.

Even though I was driving, I couldn't help but look at her; her strong, pale face, her secret smile, her eyes. She was the most beauty I had ever known, and I knew that I had to make the most of our brief time together.

The cornfields gave way to forest as the road wound up the hill. Most of the trees were evergreens, dark in the grey air, but scattered between them were bursts of sudden colour, startling reds and oranges.

How many times had I come up this hill? Saw those trees? Heard her laugh? It felt like it was all fading away. I felt like I should be struggling to savour as much as I could of every moment, but I knew it was already too late. Too far gone.

The parking lot was full, and we had to park well away from the cemetery gates. I didn't bother putting up the top. Let it rain—it didn't matter to me anymore.

We held hands across the parking lot, not speaking until we had passed through the open gates and were walking along the paved path between the orderly rows of gravestones, Henderson's past laid out, marked and remarked.

"Good turnout," I said of the cars in the lot, and the crowd we could see gathered in the distance.

She nodded. "He was well-loved."

"People came from near and far. . . ."

"He made a good life for himself," she said.

"Gone too soon."

She looked at me. "Yeah."

As we walked, the wind blew, scattering leaves orange and yellow around us. We walked through the brilliant blizzard, the sudden whorl of colour in the world of grey.

As the leaves fell to the earth, she let go of my hand and stopped.

I turned to her. "What is it?"

She stepped off the path, onto the carefully manicured lawn. "This is as far as I go, Daniel," she said, raising her hand as if to say goodbye.

I took a step toward her, but she waved me away. "You'll have to go the rest of the way on your own," she said.

"What are you talking about?" I asked, taking another step toward her. "It's right there." I gestured toward the funeral.

"You know I can't go, Danny. You know why." She reached toward me as if to touch my face, but she was too far away, just out of reach.

"Izzy, what's . . . ?"

"Thank you, Danny," she said, stepping further away from the path, across the wet grass. "Thank you for last night."

"Izzy," I cried out, stepping toward her. I reached for her, and for a moment I felt the fabric of her coat between my fingertips and then it was gone.

And she was gone.

And I was standing in the grey fall air at the foot of a grave. It was a grave I recognized, a grave I had visited dozens—hundreds— of times in the past twenty years.

Isabel Maria Scarfe
April 15, 1969 – October 14, 1985
Gone Too Soon

At the edge of the stone that was all that remained of my true friend, my first love, there was a slim bundle of carnations, withered and wet from the rain.

I had left the flowers there the week before, on the twentieth anniversary of the night that her car had left the road, flipping into the ditch, filling with water.

We had been coming back from my house, trying to beat her curfew, and she had cut the corner too close.

Gone too soon.

"Izzy," I whispered before turning away, stepping back onto the path. The crowd was close, and I could hear the voice of the priest in the cold October air.

The congregation seemed to be standing in a pool of sunlight, a patch of warmth and bright surrounded by the dark cold. Every step brought me closer to them, and I began to be able to make out individual faces in the crowd.

Colin and Alex were there, the last of the old crew still in town. They were standing with their wives, next to Sherry, who tended bar at the Bird of Paradise, and Graham, who taught at the elementary school. Frank and Jim from the press were there, scrubbed clean and dressed in black, their faces tight and lined. All of the faces were familiar, but more than I could name in the few steps I had left.

The five of them stood at the graveside.

My father, looking stoic, face lined and back hunched with his age, held my mother as she cried. My two boys, Michael and Stephen, strong little soldiers in their matching black suits, never taking their eyes from the polished wood of the coffin.

And Marie. My wife, my life, a crushed tissue in her hand, tears streaming unabated down her cheeks. I wanted to reach out to her, to try to comfort her, to tell her that I was all right.

I wanted to tell her that I had settled for nothing, that I knew now that the life we had made together was the life I was meant to have lived. I wanted to tell her all those things I had never told her in life—that she brought me joy by simply being, that our family, our life together, was more than I had ever dreamed, that just to love and be loved was a state of grace—

And as I stepped into the light, as from a dark forest into a clearing, I felt a warm wind take hold of me, lift me away from the earth, scatter me to the four directions. For a moment, just a moment, I felt myself in the sunlight, in the grass, in the leaves, in the dying and the reborn. I felt myself in the breath of my children, in my father's arms, in the tears of my wife. I felt myself in the western wind, and in the small rain.

Let it rain.

The Last Circus

I was eleven years old the day the last circus came to Henderson. It was late August, just before the Labour Day weekend, when the world would start to change and grow cold. The leaves were dry in the trees in the woods along the edges of the fields, not coloured yet, but you could feel it coming. The air was already chill in the mornings when I was out doing my chores. It was sweltering by noon, but the mornings were a hint of what was to come.

I was in the west field, far from the house, when the first of the trucks went by. I was going to bring the cows in from the pasture for milking, watching the tall grass as it whipped black lines of dew on the legs of my jeans, and probably wouldn't have even noticed the truck—there was nothing unusual about trucks with rattling, roaring engines going too fast up the road out front of the farm, farting thick blue exhaust—if not for the horn.

The whole world seemed to jump, startled by the metallic braying that started off like a distraught donkey before dissolving into a hysterical laughter that echoed in the small vee of the valley. Twisting my back faster than my legs could turn, I almost fell over as I spun toward the road.

The caravan stretched as far as I could see, all the way down to the bend at Charlie's place, maybe farther for all I knew, a ribbon of colour threading between the green of the fields.

I took a step toward the fenceline, toward the road, as the lead truck approached. It was red. You could tell the colour had once been as bright as a fire engine, but now it had faded to a rusty shade, all soft rounded lines and a bubbled hood. The truck was pulling a trailer, a battered silver Airstream, and it seemed to be barely holding together. I could hear the rattle of the frame even over the roughness of the engine.

The windshield was caked with dust; it was impossible to see the driver, but as the truck started to pull even with me, a bare arm extended from the window, gesturing in a way I couldn't quite understand. Was it a wave? A salute?

An invitation?

I jumped almost as high when the horn sounded for a second time, and I could have sworn that I heard a laugh from inside the truck as the arm pulled back in and the window rolled up partway.

But I wasn't looking at the arm, not anymore, or at the window. I was looking at the sign on the driver's side door, the rough sketch of a rounded tent, circled by the words *Zeffirelli Brothers Circus and Marvels*.

Circus and Marvels.

I forgot about the cows, forgot about everything else. I turned and ran back toward the house. The wet grass slapped at my legs, sprayed as high as my face as I ran.

The caravan unspooled alongside me, faster than I could keep up, and I kept glancing sideways at the vehicles as I ran, the ragged edge of my breath as loud as the engines. Everything I saw, every fragmentary glimpse, felt like a promise: an old VW bug painted with DayGlo flames that I just knew was full of clowns, I could picture them spilling out the doors—onetwothreetwelveninenineteen—each of them gaudier, more laugh-terrifying than the last. Another truck, this one a battered, rusted green, struggled to tow a trailer so huge I marvelled that it could move at all, the whole side of it covered with a painting of a trio of jungle cats, a lion, a tiger and a panther, garish and cartoonish, but they looked like they might leap off the truck, spring toward me without warning. A wheezing Winnebago, decorated with a painting of a beautiful woman, long red hair seeming to float behind her, the green of her eyes mirroring the scales of her tail . . .

My cousin Bob was sitting behind the kitchen table as I burst through the mudroom door. My parents had been away for almost two weeks, driving back to New Brunswick to help my grandmother. . . . Or at least that was what they said.

This is a grown-up trip, kiddo, my dad had explained, when I asked him. *You'd just be bored. Besides*, he had added, *your cousin Bob is going to stay with you while we're gone, take care of things*. It didn't really answer the question, but that was the way things were now, with my mom and dad.

"Bob! There's—"

"Cows all in?" His voice was low, slow, as he lifted the coffee-cup toward his mouth. His eyes were hidden behind his sunglasses, his hair swept back away from his face.

I couldn't contain myself. "There's a circus!" Then I realized how childish I sounded, and I felt my face start to redden. When Bob was around, I tried to imitate his slow calmness, the way he had of only saying something if he'd had a chance to think about it through some and decided it was really worth saying. I would hang around while he worked on his bike, pretending to follow along as he pointed things out to me, pretending to understand what he was talking about, but mostly just focusing on the tiniest details, like I was filing them away to give more attention to later. The flag on the side of his gas tank, the chip in the red paint from a sprayed rock. The road dust on his motorcycle boots, turning them a dusky grey. The stiffness of his jeans, the way they looked like they might stand up on their own, given half a chance. The way his leather jacket creased at his shoulders, at the back of his elbows.

Filing it all away, so I would have it when he was gone.

The one thing I did not do—not ever—when Bob was around was to act like a little kid.

I tried to pull myself together.

He set his cup—dad's cup—on the table and wiped at his moustache. "A circus?"

I nodded, not trusting myself to speak.

"What makes you say that?" He was talking even more slowly than normal, taking even longer to react than he usually did. Was he tired? Maybe he was feeling the effects of having to keep farm hours while my mom and dad were away and he was staying with me. The night before, he hadn't come in till after I was in bed.

"Look," I said, gesturing past him toward the front window.

Beyond the lawn and the front garden, a row of trucks were passing now, all of them marked with the Zeffirelli logo on their door. "Look!"

He turned slowly, but not before I saw the faintest twitches of a smile at the corner of his mouth. His voice didn't rise or change when he said, "Well. Isn't. That. Something." When he turned back around, he was grinning. "And I suppose you would like to go?"

I just nodded; there was no way I was going to even try to speak.

"Well," he said, drawing out the word. "You do have a lot of chores. . . ."

My heart stopped in my chest.

"And there's church tomorrow."

I felt like I might never breathe again.

"So I'm not sure . . ."

I blinked, hard. Why was he doing this? I couldn't make the words I was hearing match up with what I thought I knew about Bob. I couldn't make the sound of his voice square with the smile on his face. Why was he—

"Tell you what," he said slowly, as if coming to some sort of realization. "If you get your chores done."

And then it clicked. He was messing with me. I started to speak, stopped. Pushed down the grin that had bubbled up inside me once my heart had started beating again. I had to play along. A laugh threatened to burst out of me.

"And you get your clothes laid out for church."

Oh my God, it was really going to happen!

"Then we can talk about—"

"Thank you Bob!" I exploded. I felt like I was moving in every direction at once, like I wanted to run around in a circle and shout at the top of my lungs. I finally understood the way Lady, my old dog, used to feel when it was time to go for a ride in the car.

I pulled it all back in, tried to be cool, hoping that Bob hadn't noticed anything.

But his grin was even wider. He had noticed.

Placing his hands on the table, he pushed himself to his feet. "Let's get those cows in," he said, and I could hear the sound of his bootheels on the kitchen floor. "They ain't gonna milk themselves."

I had never been to a circus.

I mean, I had read about them in books and comics, but I had never actually been to one for real. I knew what to expect, but I had no idea what to expect.

I spent the morning in a blur of excitement and confusion: I did my chores as fast as I could, driving the cows to the barn at almost a running pace, throwing hay bales down from the loft as Bob milked, collecting eggs from the chickens and scattering feed, standing still for just a moment as they thrashed and puffed and clucked all around me.

I had finished all the reading and worksheets that my teachers had given me for the summer, so I didn't have to worry about that. I showered without needing to be asked, taking actual time to wash my hair and scrub myself, not just standing in the rainstorm, as my mom called what I usually did.

I laid out my church clothes on the chair in front of my desk, careful to line up the creases and folds just right so there wouldn't be any wrinkles the next morning.

When I got back down to the kitchen—dressed, hair brushed— Bob was just getting in from the barn, shaking out his leather jacket and draping it over the back of a chair.

"I've finished my chores," I said, trying to keep my voice calm and steady. "And my clothes are laid out."

"You know the circus isn't until tonight, right?" he said, adjusting his jacket so it hung evenly. Not looking at me.

I felt like I was vibrating, like everything inside me was speeding up, like I might not be able to hold myself together much longer.

When Bob turned toward me, his face was curiously flat, expressionless. "Can you grab something for me?" His voice not giving anything away. "Just on the top of the fridge."

I shuffled a couple of steps. I wasn't tall enough to see onto the top of the fridge, but I could reach. My fingers brushed the cool curve of the blue mixing bowl, and I looked at him questioningly.

"Should be an envelope."

I patted my fingertips along the top of the fridge, its cool white smoothness with just a hint of warmth underneath, warmth and the faint vibration of motor and fan.

When I felt the roughness of the paper, the envelope, I slid it to the edge so I could pick it up. I extended the envelope toward Bob, but he shook his head. "It's not for me," he said.

My name was written on the front of the envelope, my mother's loopy handwriting as familiar as my own cramped scrawl. The envelope wasn't sealed, the flap tucked into the opening, easy to wiggle free. Something moved inside me, an almost anxious sense of excitement, anticipation that felt almost like dread.

I looked up at Bob. His features slipped into his usual easy smile.

"For real?"

He just grinned as I slipped two orange tickets into my hand. They were thick, thicker than the art paper at school, and printed with the same logo I had seen on the doors of the caravan: Zeffirelli Brothers Circus and Marvels, over the words *Henderson Agricultural Grounds* and today's date.

7:30 pm.

I couldn't pull my eyes away.

"But . . ."

It didn't make sense.

"How . . ."

Bob waved his hands in the air, whispering "Magic."

It had to be. My parents had been gone for weeks, and the circus had only come to town this morning, so how had they—

"It was in the papers, you goof," Bob said, shaking his head.

"What?"

"The circus. There have been ads for it in the paper for the last couple of weeks, and tickets for sale at the Shop Rite." He watched me as I tried to put everything together. "Haven't your friends been talking about it? I would have thought everyone was going mental."

Jaws clamped tight around my heart.

Bob was looking at me. "Didn't your friends say anything?"

I started to say something like *I don't—* or *What friends?* but stopped myself. "I guess they hadn't heard about it either," I lied. "Maybe their parents wanted to surprise them, too."

He nodded slowly. "Maybe," he said, looking at me closely, like he was noticing something he hadn't seen before.

I looked back down at the tickets, rubbing my fingers over the symbol.

Bob was already on the bike, wiping at a spot on the gas tank, as I fumbled with the helmet's strap and buckle. I took a step back from Bob's bike and turned slightly away. I didn't want him to see me.

"You ready?" he called back to me, the engine sliding into a smooth rumble, somewhere between a purr and a roar.

"Yeah, I—" The buckle slipped around the strap and I pulled it snug, with a sharp sense of relief.

"Hop on," he said, without looking back.

It only took me a moment to straddle the motorcycle, hopping slightly on one foot to plant myself on the small seat behind him.

"You good?" He turned partway, and I saw a glimpse of the garage through the right lens of his sunglasses.

I lifted my thumb toward him. *Cool*, I thought.

"Hold on," he said, and I looped my arms partway around him, pulling in close to his back. He smelled of sweat and gasoline, aftershave and leather, and a high, kind of skunky smokiness. Bob didn't wear a helmet, and his hair tickled my nose a bit.

Gravel crunched under the tires as he turned the motorcycle in a loose curve, and we drove up the driveway, pausing for a moment—not really coming to a stop—before turning onto the road.

"You . . . long way?" I couldn't really make out what Bob was saying over the engine noise and through my helmet, but I risked another thumbs-up, my other hand tight to his side.

Bob turned the bike away from town, and the gravel gave way to the smoothness of the asphalt.

Oh, the long way.

The wind pulled and tugged at my jacket, rough against the skin of my face as the bike picked up speed. I pulled a little closer to Bob, but not because I was scared or anything.

I was the furthest thing from scared it was possible to be.

I hadn't been on the bike with Bob very often—just a few times in the couple of years since he had got it—but every time it felt the same. The wind, the speed, felt like a surging in the pit of my stomach, a rush that spread through my bloodstream, into my heart, then down to my fingers and toes. It felt electric, like that moment you lose control laughing, but extended, dizzying, for the entire length of the ride.

And it wasn't just the speed, the sense of flight; it was the way being on the back of the bike seemed to open a new window onto a world I thought I knew.

I had spent my whole life in the fields that now zipped past us in a blaze of green and brown, individual rows of corn disappearing into a high emerald sea, gardens blurring into indistinct shades. I had spent my whole life on these roads, either walking along the crest of the ditch or riding my bike on the narrow shoulder. I'd even ridden my bike around the mountain once or twice on my own, budgeting a whole afternoon, pushing my bike up the hills, holding tight to the handlebars and touching the brakes to keep control on the downhills, conscious always of the sheer drop on one side, stopping at the old cemetery to mark the half-way point of the ride with a snack and a chance to catch my breath. But I'd never really felt the road itself, the gentle rolls and curves, the pebbly velvet of the asphalt surface.

The world had seemed so big, so daunting, but on the bike the twenty-minute walk to the Hi Way Market was over in a blink. On Bob's bike, the uphills seemed to disappear, and I whooped as we roared down the hills, the bike hugging the curves of the road. I didn't pay any attention to the drop-offs. I trusted Bob more than I trusted myself. He would never let me down—that was one of the only things in my life that I was sure of.

The old cemetery flashed by us in a blur, the slope a swath of green cut into the forested mountain side, and it was over. From here, it was all flat ground, straight roads, sharp corners to the fair grounds.

I wanted to tap Bob on the shoulder, gesture that I wanted to keep riding, that I didn't want that feeling to stop. I never wanted that feeling to stop.

And then I saw the circus.

❧

I was born in Henderson. I grew up on the farm my father grew up on. Bob started taking me to 4H meetings when I was five, calling me his "little cousin" and referring to me as one of the "Future Farmers of Henderson" like the 4H sign said. I basked in the glow of his words like corn in a June rain.

When he stopped going to the meetings, I stopped going as well. Mom and Dad offered to drive me, but I said no. It wouldn't have been the same without him there.

Nothing would be.

The 4H meetings were held in the Livestock Pavilion, where they had bingo every Wednesday and Sunday, and roller-skating for the teenagers every Friday night. It was a huge building, full of echoes and the smell of old hay, on the back corner of the Agricultural Grounds.

I went with Bob to the Agricultural Grounds for those meetings once a week for years. The school bus drove right past them, before school and after. The Grounds, the Pavilion, the Agricultural Hall, on the front corner, closest to the road—I knew these places almost as well as I knew the farm.

And I knew them, even when, once a year, everything changed. The third weekend of September, every year, was the Harvest Festival. After school on the Friday, everything would look the same through the bus windows. Maybe a few extra cars in the lot, but nothing out of the ordinary. But overnight, the Ag Grounds would be transformed, and on Saturday morning, when we would bring the car in early to get a good parking spot before the parade, there would be a midway, with a Ferris Wheel and a Zipper. There would be games and a haunted house. The stage would be draped with bunting and decorated with corn, ready for the crowning of the Harvest King, and a smaller stage would be set up next to a huge white tent, where the bands would play for the beer garden. They needed that tent to shade the people in the beer garden from the sun: it never rained on festival day.

The midway, the sun—it was all just part of the magic of the Festival every year. And it wasn't just me that felt it: for the whole week leading up to it, the whole school thrummed like the feeling you get in your chest when you touch an electric fence.

It was the best day of the year.

But even all that magic paled next to the very first glimpse I had of the circus from the back of Bob's motorcycle.

The fencing along the road had been covered in paintings, bright colour stretching as far as the eye could see, obscuring the lower edge of the vista with a make-shift mural of . . . what had the sign on the trucks called them?

Marvels.

I had to force myself not to react, not to squeeze any tighter with my legs, not to make a sound.

But I wanted to.

Oh, how I wanted to.

Amid the swirling colours of the mural, a man with a black goatee slid a sword down his throat, his blue eyes glaring out from the paint. The mermaid's eyes—green—were warmer, almost inviting. There was a fire eater, and a pair of trapeze artists. A little girl in what looked like a shiny silver bathing suit sat with her legs wrapped around her shoulders, while a wire walker balanced high above the center ring. A lion roared, his mouth so wet and red I almost thought I could hear him. There was a man with tattoos all over his face, and a mass of snakes that seemed to squirm as I watched them. And there were clowns everywhere, pale faces and bright mouths, lurking in the paint like they were hiding, like they might jump out at any moment.

I wanted to keep going, like if Bob just kept driving, the murals would keep unspooling, an endless, constant revelation of colours, of wonders. All we had to do was keep moving.

But with a sudden lean that made my stomach feel like it was going to slip out, Bob turned the bike into a gap between the images, into one of the driveways into the parking lot. The tires bit and spat gravel as we left the road.

I had to hold myself in check as we crossed the parking lot. In the distance I could see the outline of trucks and structures, the crest of a tent bright against the sky. The air was laced with hints of music and popcorn.

I had always been jealous of the way Bob walked, as slow and thoughtful as the way he talked, steady and cool, like nothing ever rattled him. Like nothing was worth rushing over.

But some things *were* worth rushing for, and it was all I could do to slow down, to fight that desire to run.

"You excited?" Bob asked, as if he could tell what I was feeling. His boots crunched in the gravel.

I had to actually look back at him to answer. "It's all right, I guess." I forced myself to slow down even more, to even my strides with his.

"Oh, yeah?" A smile played underneath his moustache, there for an instant, then gone again. But I could see it in his eyes. "We could just skip it. Work our way through the rest of the To Do list your parents left."

"I guess," I said, playing along. "But mom and dad did go to all the trouble of getting the tickets." Trying to make my voice sound like I was reluctant, but willing to sacrifice myself in order to be polite.

"I suppose," he said, and the smile came back, for good this time.

His grin broadened when we got to the gate.

"John," he said, slapping his hand into the palm of the man at the entry, shaking his hand vigorously. "How'd you get this gig?"

John Horvath—that's who it was—smiled just as broadly. "What, you didn't run away and join the circus?" He was tall, wide-shouldered, a small black apron with heavy pockets loose around his hips.

"Nah," Bob said. "Who's got time for that?" Obviously a dig, but a friendly one.

John nodded like Bob had said something smart. "I got ya, I got ya." He glanced toward me. "Nah. I was at the Triple Crown the other night and this guy came in, asking if anybody wanted a day's work, cash on the barrelhead." He shrugged. "I was gonna give you a call, but his list filled up pretty quick." He sounded apologetic.

Bob shook his head, shook it away. "So what they got you doing, taking tickets and stamping hands?"

John grinned and reached into the main pocket of his apron, pulling out a single-hole punch, like the ones we had at school. "You know it," he said, clicking the punch closed and open a couple of times.

"That's quite the responsibility."

"Screw you," John said, but you could tell he didn't really mean it. "That's just now," he added. "They had us in at first light, setting up the grounds, hanging the posters—" and he gestured toward the fence, that endless row of paintings, "—putting up the tents."

As he spoke, I lifted my gaze above his head. There was a temporary wall behind him, painted with the Zeffirelli logo, that blocked the view, but over the top of it I could see the tops of several tents, bright, multi-coloured, rounded peaks, several smaller ones surrounding a single huge tent.

My heart felt like it was going to explode in my chest.

"It looks like someone's excited," John said, and when I lowered my eyes, he was staring right at me.

"This is my cousin," Bob said.

"Course he is," John said, then he extended the punch toward me. "You got a ticket?"

I had a momentary panic. Had we remembered to bring the tickets? What if they were still on the fridge? Would we have to—

But Bob reached into his back pocket and pulled out the two orange cardboard rectangles, passing me one. "Here you go."

My face started to go hot as I extended my ticket toward John.

"Let's see here," he said as he took it from me. "Mr. Zeffirelli told us we had to do this exactly right." He slid the ticket between the jaws of the hole punch, squinting a little and biting his lip.

"There's really a Zeffirelli?" Bob asked. I didn't understand the question; of course there was a Mr. Zeffirelli. Who else would—

"Of course there is," John said. "He's the ringmaster." John gestured toward the murals, toward the man with the goatee and top hat. "That's him."

The hole punch clicked closed, and open again, and a small orange fragment fluttered to the ground.

"There you go," he said, handing me back the ticket. A star-shaped hole had been punched out of the very middle of the circle of the logo.

John was grinning, like this was as exciting for him as it was for me. "You can get a stamp if you want to leave and come back."

"Thank you," I said quietly, clutching the ticket.

He tipped an imaginary hat at me before turning his attention to Bob. "So, are you going in?"

Bob nodded, cocked his head toward me. "His folks asked me to keep an eye on him while they're away."

I could hear a shrug that Bob didn't really give, and my stomach fell between my shoes.

"Right," John said, and took Bob's ticket. "Hey, listen, when do you head out?"

I looked at the ground. Somewhere in the distance, I could hear the click of the hole punch.

Bob glanced at me. "Next Sunday," he said.

"Not gonna have much use for your bike on the prairies all winter," said Bob.

"I'm not leaving it with you."

They laughed.

The gravel was thin, pressed hard into the earth, littered with cigarette butts and the fragments from the tickets. A few feet away a dried clump of dog shit had been kicked off to the grassy edge.

"You're not gonna have much time for riding anyway."

"I don't figure so."

"Hitting the books pretty hard."

"That's the way it's done, I hear."

"Well, listen—" At the shift in his voice I looked up. John was looking at the ground now, shifting uneasily from foot to foot. "If I don't see you . . ."

Bob shook his head. "You'll see me. Before I leave." He nodded, as if to mark the words. "I'll be around."

"Okay," John said, nodding himself. "Here you go, then." He handed Bob his ticket. "Welcome to Zeffirelli's."

Bob brought his hand down on the back of my neck, squeezing it gently.

"Shall we?"

I didn't say anything as we went through the gate.

⟨

The first thing I noticed about the circus was the smell: the high, sharp rank of shit. Growing up on a farm, in the country, I was familiar with the cloying sweetness of pig shit, the warm musk of cow, the clear force of horse, even the sharp, ammonia smell of chicken. I had grown up with those smells. They smelled like home to me. This was something different, something foreign. Something new.

I wrinkled my nose and Bob caught my eye as I glanced around, trying to figure it out.

"Lion?" he asked, grinning. "Tiger? Bear?" He wrinkled his whole face, as if suddenly overwhelmed with the smell. "Oh my." He waited for me to react, to say something.

I forced my face to stillness.

"Listen," he said, stopping, forcing me to stop. "I know you're not happy about me leaving."

I focused on looking at the rough upper edge of his beard, low on his cheeks, almost but not quite making eye contact, almost but not quite looking away.

"It's not forever," he said. "I'll be back for the Harvest Festival. That's less than a month. Then Thanksgiving. And Christmas." He reached out and touched my shoulder, held his hand there. "You're gonna be all right," he said, leaning in toward me. "And hey, maybe you can come see me at school." He tried to make it sound exciting.

I tried not to react, but he must have seen something in my face.

"I've gotta go," he said. "I can't stay here my whole life. There's such a big world out there." He looked up, and around, and his motion forced me to do the same. "It's a world of wonders," he said, and it sounded like something caught in his throat. "You'll see," he said. "When you're older."

I shook my head sharply. "Don't do that," I said, before I could stop myself. "Don't make it sound like I don't get it because I'm just a kid. Don't make it sound like I don't understand things."

He looked at me like he couldn't believe the words that were coming out of my mouth. I couldn't either.

"I know you need to get out of here," I said, giving up on even trying to stop myself. "I know that school's just an excuse. You just want to leave."

His eyes flickered.

"And I know you're not going to be back for the Harvest Festival, or Thanksgiving. You're not gonna drive fifteen hours to spend a night here before you have to turn around and go back."

He looked like he was doing what I had been doing, forcing himself not to react.

"Maybe you'll come back at Christmas, maybe not. You're gonna make friends at school. You're gonna disappear."

I had seen it happen before. When people left, they didn't come back. Sure, they might come out for the Harvest Festival, or to see their folks, but that was it. My babysitter, Chantelle, had promised to come back, the same way Bob was. I'd only seen her twice in the three years since she had graduated and moved away.

People disappeared. They left, and they didn't come back. They promised, and they lied.

"Everybody disappears," I said. "Nobody tells the truth."

He shook his head. "Hey, that's not—"

"What are my mom and dad really doing?"

He stopped, and his mouth and eyes widened.

"I know they're not on vacation. If they were on vacation, we all would have gone together. So, what? They're gonna come back and tell me that they've decided they don't want to be married anymore? That Dad's not going to live with us anymore?"

The expression on his face, shocked and sad, told me that I was right. About everything.

And I had wanted so desperately to be wrong.

"So don't tell me I'm too young to understand things. I understand things just fine."

I stalked away, and I knew he wouldn't follow.

There were people. Lots of them. People everywhere. I hadn't really noticed them while Bob and I were talking, but once I walked away, it was like I was swimming upstream, bumping and jostling with every step.

I had scurried away from Bob as fast as I could, without breaking into a run. I didn't want to call any attention to myself; I didn't want anyone to notice me at all. I kept my head hunched low, my body in a tight bundle, my eyes focused on the crushed brown grass, the ruts already worn where people were walking back and forth.

Near one of the shooting galleries, Casey Williams turned toward me, smacking Jeff Gilles on the shoulder to get his attention. And then the whole group of them turned to look at me, and I could feel myself shrinking.

"Hey farmer boy," someone called.

I ducked behind one of the trailers that had been pulled onto one of the baseball diamonds. Its side panels were opened up to reveal a carnival game, a shooting gallery with moving targets and plush prizes. I checked inside the dugout to be sure it was empty, then went inside, tucking myself into the corner furthest from the grinding motor on the back of the truck, the one that moved the targets, belching blue clouds of gassy smoke into the August sky.

Settling onto the bench, I pressed my back into the corner, against the concrete wall, and pulled my knees into my chest.

No one would find me here.

Not that anyone would be looking.

For a long time I sat there, thinking about what I had said to Bob. Wondering how it was possible to know something without even knowing you knew it.

I had known for a while that Bob wasn't going to come back, not in any meaningful way. Once he packed up his motorcycle and headed east, he would be gone. If he came back, he would just be a guest, someone visiting. He wouldn't be around the way he always had been. It would be like the 4H all over again, the way he had slipped out of the fabric of things. He wouldn't be there after school anymore, or on Saturday afternoons, the sound of his bike a thunder in the driveway that I could hear no matter where I was on the farm.

How many more times would I hear that sound, run to where I could see him, wave until I caught his attention?

He had looked so surprised when I said what I did. Was he surprised that I knew, or had he never really thought about it?

Gone. Already gone.

Like my parents. My dad.

I don't know that I had put that together before the words were coming out of my mouth, but the surprise on Bob's face then had been clear: I wasn't supposed to know. Not yet.

But it had been obvious for a long time. There had been too many nights I had woken to the sound of raised voices, distant, a floor away, the words indistinguishable but the tone clear. I lay in bed awake those nights, eyes wide, my head buried in the pillow, trying to drown out the sound, until the voices stopped, until I heard the creaking tread of feet on the stairs. Too many mornings coming downstairs to the hints that something was wrong: pillows out of place on the couch, the coffee table moved. Like someone had slept there, but they didn't want anyone to know.

They didn't want me to know.

Too many times I had come into the living room, or kitchen, and the conversation stopped so quickly I could practically hear their mouths slapping shut, an almost electrical silence filling the room, crackling around us until one of them asked something like "So how was school?" Forced smiles slipping over their faces like masks.

My parents were splitting up.

Bob was leaving.

Nothing was ever going to be the same.

It was almost too much to bear.

Closing my eyes, I slumped my head back against the cool concrete roughness of the dugout wall.

"And what have we here?"

The voice was so close to my ear it seemed almost like a whispering inside my head. I jumped, practically pushing myself up the wall. My eyes flashed open as my neck scraped along the concrete, my hands flailing out to push away whoever had whispered in my ear.

But there was no one there, no one within the range of my weak, wheeling arms.

A man was at the far end of the dugout, a smile breaking through the darkness of his goatee.

"Mr.—" It seemed too surreal to possibly be true. "—Zeffirelli?"

The smile widened, and the man took a small bow, the tails of his black suit jacket swishing dramatically around his legs.

"At your service," he said, tipping his top hat toward me.

"I'm sorry," I said haltingly. I didn't know why I was apologizing; it seemed like the right thing to do. "I just—"

He shook his head, cutting me off. "No need to explain," he said. "We all need to take a moment to ourselves sometimes." With a shrug of his shoulders and a twitch of his arms he straightened the sleeves of his jacket. "A world of wonders can be overwhelming."

I looked down at the scuffed, dusty ground.

"Ah," Zeffirelli said, and I heard him moving. When I looked up, he had taken a couple of steps closer to me. "But it's not that, is it?"

I shook my head, and the corners of his mouth turned downward.

"Well," he said, snapping the fingers of his right hand. "That is most unfortunate." Between the fingers he had snapped he held the stem of a carnation, the flower so red it looked almost like a rose. "No, that's not right," he said. He was looking at the flower, but I couldn't tell if he was talking to it, or to me.

I couldn't take my eyes off the flower, transfixed as he slipped the stem into the front pocket of his jacket, shifting it until it met some sort of internal test. It looked like a corsage.

He brushed his lapels down with both hands. When he lifted his right hand, he seemed surprised to see a handkerchief dangling from between his thumb and forefinger.

"Oh," he said, as if genuinely flummoxed. "That's—"

I couldn't help but smile.

"That's more like it," he said, tossing the handkerchief in the air. Then he snapped his fingers, and the white square of cloth vanished.

I couldn't believe what I was seeing. My eyes kept moving, back and forth, between the flower in his pocket and the space in the air where the handkerchief had disappeared, my stomach roiling and surging, my heart beating in my chest like I had been running.

He didn't seem to notice, was patting his pockets as if looking for something.

"Now, where did I—" He reached into his pants pockets and turned them out, limp and white and empty.

I wanted to say something but I didn't trust myself to speak, had no idea what sounds my mouth might make if I dared to open it.

"Ah, here we are," he said, reaching toward me with an open, empty hand. He snapped his fingers again to reveal a gold coin, which he extended toward me. "Here," he said. "This is for you."

I didn't take the coin. I didn't take my eyes off it, either.

He looked at me for a moment, then nodded. "Ah," he said, a little sadly. "Of course." The hand withdrew, and I watched as he slipped the coin into his jacket pocket. "I should know better."

The disappearance of the coin caused a pang in me, in my stomach, my chest, and I wanted to reach out for it, to ask for it. But I didn't do anything except wish for that moment back, for another chance to make that decision.

To make things turn out another way.

"Of course you've been told not to take gifts from people you don't know. Candy from strangers. Rides from drivers who pull over to offer you a lift." He nodded deeply, repeatedly. "I understand entirely. Your parents have done a good job."

Something flickered in his eyes as he looked at me, a response to something in my face.

"But there's something I bet your parents didn't teach you," he said, his voice low. He took another step toward me.

"What?" I asked.

He smiled, then snapped his fingers again. The gold coin appeared in his hand, like he had snatched it out of thin air. "Sometimes—" He snapped again, and the coin disappeared. "You have to take a chance to trust."

I looked between his hand and his face.

"Trust yourself." He snapped, and the coin reappeared. "Because life is too short to live in fear." Snap, and the coin was gone. "And opportunities—" Snap. Coin. "Are like circuses." Snap. Gone. "They're here." Snap. "Then gone." Snap.

He waved his hand in the air, as if to indicate that the coin was well and truly gone this time. Inside me, something broke.

"I know that it's a hard world," Zeffirelli said softly, his lips creasing in something between a smile and a frown.

I hesitated, then nodded.

"It's up to us to find what joy we can, where we can," he said, nodding. "It's often hiding in the most obvious of places." His eyes shone as he straightened up. "Promise me you'll enjoy the circus," he said, meeting my eyes. "At least give yourself that."

I looked back at the ground. "I'll try," I said, with no idea how that might actually work.

When I looked back at him, he was frowning. "I suppose that will have to do," he said, starting to turn away. "Oh," he added, stopping. "Perhaps this will help."

He snapped his fingers one last time as he turned and stepped out of the dugout. Then he walked away, holding himself tall and straight as he turned around the back of the wagon.

I felt a strange warmth in my pocket, an unfamiliar heaviness.

My hand shook as I pushed it into my pocket, as I pulled out the gold coin.

It felt like the ground might give way underneath me.

（

I couldn't have been there for very long, but in that time, the world seemed to have changed. Stepping out from the dugout, stepping around the motor and the trailer, clutching the coin in my right hand, I had to stop. Though the high sun had given away to lengthening afternoon shadows, everything seemed brighter somehow. The lights on the games, the flags twitching in the warm breeze, the paintings on the sides of the trailers, all seemed to sparkle and pulse, so vibrant they left streaks of colour on the insides of my eyelids whenever I blinked.

The air was warm, but not hot, and thick with the smells of the circus: buttery popcorn. diesel, sweet cotton candy, the familiar richness of barbecuing chicken, all laced faintly with an ever-present background tang. I had no idea what animal made that.

Tightening my grip on the coin, I set forth to figure it out.

The crowds were heavier now, the passages between the tents and trailers congested and loud, but it didn't seem to bother me anymore. I slipped into the river of people and let it carry me along, content to let myself drift among the smiling faces and laughing voices. It felt like everyone in town was there, the fairgrounds even more packed than they were for the Harvest Festival.

Unlike the festival, though, no one seemed to know where they were going. Because the Harvest Festival had been happening every September for over a hundred years, everyone knew their way around: the shortcuts to avoid the midway, the washrooms with the shortest lines. The prize fruits and vegetables, baking and crafts were always in the Ag Hall, the 4H animals in the Pavillion, the demolition derby in the gravel lot where people parked for softball during the summer. The whole thing was an institution, a world as familiar to everyone as anything else in town.

But this was different. There might have been circuses in Henderson before, but not within my memory, and everyone was wending aimlessly through the sudden unfamiliarity. They seemed to be enjoying the strangeness, eyes questing and wide, full of questions.

Questions and . . .

Wonder.

That was what Zeffirelli had described in the dugout, and now that I was looking for it, I could see it everywhere. Not just in the faces of the little kids, who were gaping around like their minds had exploded, but on the faces of their parents and grandparents too, in the expressions of the teenagers, usually too cool to reveal anything even remotely genuine.

And more than seeing it, I could feel it, too, a warmth that spread through me, from the pit of my stomach to the tips of my toes, a warmth that seemed to concentrate in the bones and muscles of my face, leaving me uncertain if I wanted to laugh or cry. So I just drifted, my fingers locked around the coin in my pocket.

A crowd of people were gathered in the center of the gravel parking lot, in a rough ring in the middle of the circled wagons. A man in a long red coat, with a top hat and a luxurious moustache—he looked like he could have been Zeffirelli's brother—had stepped toward the back of one of the wagons, reached for the heavy latch, then stopped, his hand poised in the air.

"Step back," he shouted, staring at the crowd. "Step back, all of you. I can't guarantee your safety."

As we all took several uncertain steps back, glancing at one another in confusion, he flung the doors of the wagon open.

For a moment, there was just darkness inside—shadows and a sense of something lurking there, something watching. Then the lions spilled out through the door, their golden fur flashing and burning in the late afternoon light.

I almost stumbled, stepping backward, unable to tear my eyes away. When I had looked at them through the bars of the trailer a while earlier, the lions had been draped across the hay-strewn floor, eyes half-open, their bodies strong and powerful, but limp and soft. They had looked like barn cats, sleeping out a hot afternoon in the shade of the hay loft, occasionally opening a lazy eye to check on the world around them.

But now, bursting out of the trailer . . .

A startled cry ran through the crowd as the male reared his head back and roared, his mane shivering. He roared again, and someone screamed, and the whip that had appeared in the trainer's hand, like a flower, or a coin, cracked with a sound like a gunshot.

And then, as if on cue, the music started, an explosion of hurdy-gurdy and tuba that seemed to be coming from all around us. We all spun in place, trying to see what was going on without losing sight of the lions.

A band of clowns was marching into the circle from between two trailers.

No—marching is the wrong word.

The band, led by a tall man in white-face with a blood smile and fluorescent green hair, carrying a tasselled staff, lurched into view, their movements mirroring the chaotic, cacophonous sounds of their instruments.

They came right for us. It looked like they were going to crash right into the crowd, like they didn't even see us, but at the last moment the conductor wove and led the band around us, calling out, "Come on, everybody! The show is about to begin!" as they careened in the direction of the big top.

The crowd surged behind them, laughing and shrieking, lurching in step and sing-shouting along to the music. Everyone was focused on the clowns, on the tent, utterly caught up in what was happening, and what was about to happen. Everyone had forgotten about the lions.

Except me.

As the crowd dispersed, I edged forward, closer to the lion tamer. Still far enough away—I thought—that I was safe, but close enough to smell the heavy musk that wafted from their every movement like an African breeze.

The lions were pacing now, walking calmly in a small circle around the trainer, who held his whip in the air like an antenna, not moving it.

He didn't need to.

With one word in a language I didn't recognize, a single sharp syllable, the lions turned and began to circle him in the other direction, no hesitation, no resistance, a seamless tumble of golden fur and another wave of that smell.

Another word, and the lions stopped in place and sat, their attention entirely focused on the trainer's face, ignoring the whip hand altogether.

The lion tamer smiled, lowered the whip, making a sound that seemed affectionate, almost maternal. It was easy to imagine him stepping forward to scratch the big cats behind their ears.

Instead, he lifted his head and looked directly at me, meeting my eye. He tipped his hat to me, the way Zeffirelli had done in the dugout. "You should go," he said, placing the hat back on his head. "But I will see you soon."

With one last look at the lions, his words echoing faintly in my ears, I turned and started for the big top, and ran directly into Bob, face first into his leather jacket.

"Whoa, there," he said.

The jacket smelled like him: leather and aftershave and smoke.

"Hey," he said, a moment later, like it had taken him a second to realize it was me. "I've been looking for you."

"Come on," I said, doing everything but pull on his arm to get him to follow me. "We have to go."

He fell into step beside me, slightly back. "What's going on?"

"It's about to start!"

The grounds were almost empty, just a few people rushing toward the red and white tent.

"I know," he said, "That's why I was looking for you. I saw the clowns—"

"Did you see the lions?" I asked, too impatient to let him finish.

He wrinkled his face and nodded. "Yeah," he said, in a tone almost like regret.

"Weren't they cool?" Practically vibrating with excitement.

"Did you really think so?" He looked down at the ground. "I thought they looked . . . sad."

I slowed. "Sad?"

He shook his head. "It's nothing," he said, but his face was twisted like he had smelled something bad.

We walked in silence for a few steps before he asked, "What about you? You doin' okay?"

For a moment, I wasn't sure what he meant. Then I remembered what had happened at the gate. "Yeah, I'm fine."

And I was surprised to realize that I really was. I hadn't forgotten about mom and dad, or about Bob leaving, but I didn't seem to have any trace of the desperate, drowning feeling that I had had earlier in the afternoon.

Mostly, I just wanted to get inside the big top.

"Are you sure?" His voice creaked a little, something I don't think I had ever heard before. "I was looking for you. . . ."

I nodded. "It's all right," I said. Then, gesturing, "Come on."

It was only when we started walking again that I realized I was still clutching the coin Zeffirelli had given me in my right hand.

I wondered, for a moment, how long I had been holding it. And why I hadn't noticed.

The big top was at the centre of the maze of trailers like a beacon. There were still scattered people rushing toward it; we weren't the last ones. I could hear the clowns' music from across the field, and so long as the music was playing, the real show wouldn't start.

Or so I assumed.

"Come on," I urged Bob, as we passed the entrance to the side show, the golden rope and the red-beaded curtain and the sign that read *No Minors*. The man on the stool beside the rope tipped his hat to me as we passed.

There was one entrance to the big top, a seam in the side of the tent that had been pulled open and tied back, wide enough to allow just two people at a time to pass through side by side.

Bob and I joined the back of the crowd waiting to enter, a solid mass of heat and the smell of sweat. As more people filled in behind us, we were pushed forward, my nose almost pressed against Mr. Wilkes' sweaty back in front of me.

He turned back and glared at me as I jostled him. I smiled helplessly, lifting my heads to gesture that somebody had shoved me from behind, that there was nothing I could do.

Bob reached out to steady me, rocked as someone shoved him. "For fuck's sake," he muttered, drawing a glare from Mrs. Wilkes. Bob didn't even bother with a smile, just glared right back. Then he half-turned toward me and started to smile as the crowd lurched again.

I reached out toward him, but this time the mass of people didn't ebb, pushing me forward almost to the edge of the tent before my feet touched the ground again.

I felt Bob's hand on my shoulder. "Are you okay?" he mouthed, as we lurched forward again.

I nodded, trying to quell the feeling of panic rising in me as we passed into the big top. The crowd narrowed and funnelled between the edges of two sets of bleachers. It was dim and hot, and I couldn't see anything except the shuddering mass of people around me and a faint glow in the distance.

The crowd bunched again, and I bit back a cry as I was carried several feet along in the dark, caught up in a spring-swollen river like deadfall. And then the forward motion stopped, and again the pressure from the people behind me pressed me into the man in front of me, not Mr. Wilkes now but someone I didn't have a chance to recognize before I was crushed up against them.

The pressure was too much. I couldn't breathe. I couldn't speak. I tried to turn. I struggled to free my hands, to bring them up, to try to fight free, but I couldn't—

The people in front of me lurched forward, the crowd dispersing to either side as it reached the end of the bleachers and people broke off in both directions to find places to sit.

Bob reached out for me, caught my shoulder. "Are you all right?" His face was caught in an expression of incredulous disbelief, hot and flushed, his hair flipped over onto his forehead, sticking there.

"I'm okay." I nodded as he reached up to flip his hair back.

I started to do the same, unconsciously mirroring his gesture, when I noticed that both my hands were empty.

I had dropped the coin.

People bumped into me and someone cursed as I stopped, digging my fingers deep into my pockets, knowing there was no hope.

The gold coin was gone.

"Are these all right?" Bob asked, pointing at two empty spots on the bleachers, about halfway up, off to one side.

I didn't say anything as I checked all of my pockets again, front and back, patting outside my jeans, hoping to feel the round outline, then digging in, hoping despite the fact I knew they were empty.

"Hey," he said, pointing at the seats.

"Sure," I said, following him past the two people sitting at the end of the row close to the aisle. The seats were fine; the tent was so full we didn't have a lot of options, and it didn't really matter anyway. Nothing did.

"Are you all right?" he asked again, quietly, as I squeezed into the spot next to him, Mr. Abbot radiating heat against my other side. He looked so worried, so concerned, that I wanted to say something to comfort him.

"I'm okay," I lied.

His face didn't change, and his eyes remained focused directly on mine.

"My stomach," I said weakly, gesturing vaguely in the air as if I didn't want to say anything else.

He nodded and almost smiled, as if the idea—or the fact of an explanation—was somehow comforting. "Gotcha," he said. "Too much junk food?"

I shrugged half-heartedly. "I guess."

He patted my knee. "You'll be all right."

It didn't seem that way to me. At that moment, it felt like I might never be all right again.

Losing the coin felt like a hole opening up inside me, a sucking darkness that seemed to lurk in the pit of my stomach. It made me feel like I was going to throw up, like maybe I hadn't entirely lied to Bob. It just wasn't junk food. It felt like I was full of poison, the black jelly of everything I had lost—my parents, Bob, the coin. It made me want to vomit, and to lash out. Every time Mr. Abbot shifted, the hot, sweaty length of him pressing into me, I wanted to scream, to punch him.

Or curl up under the bleachers and cry and hope that no one would ever find me and hope that someone would come.

Bob patted my knee again, and left his hand there. It was all I could do not to cry.

And then the lights went out, and the beam of a single spotlight cut through the big top.

"Ladies and gentlemen," Zeffirelli cried out from the center of the ring, "boys and girls, welcome to Zeffirelli's world of wonders!"

The crowd roared as he tipped his hat, and I leaned back in my place.

He looked almost the same, but off, somehow. Different.

Was this the same man I had met in the dugout?

He was wearing the same clothes, but in the brightness of the spotlight I could see how tattered they were, the thin, shiny patches at his elbows and knees, the thready roughness of the lapels. The spotlight seemed to magnify him: it was like I was close enough to study the thin, patchiness of his goatee, the sag of his neck, the grey mostly hidden in his hair shining like a beacon.

Mostly, though, the difference was in his eyes, flat and dull and listless as he spoke, like he was reading from a script. There was little trace of the man I had met earlier, the man who had made a handkerchief appear out of thin air, a coin—

A coin that I had lost.

My heart fell. Maybe it was my fault – he had made the coin appear, and I, in my stupid clumsiness, had made it disappear.

"I must warn you," he was saying, "please, no sudden moves or loud noises, these are wild animals, here direct from darkest Africa . . ." A ripple of excitement ran through the audience. "Please welcome Franco and the wild cats of the Serengeti!"

On cue, the spotlight snapped to darkness, and light filled the back of the ring where a doorway in the canvas wall gaped suddenly open, revealing the lions that—

But were these the same lions? They couldn't be. These lions were slow and docile, stringy and thin, their fur matted in places, rubbed raw in others. The moved with a sloppy lope, heads low, eyes flat in the bright lights.

They looked . . . broken.

My eyes burned as I struggled to my feet.

Bob twisted to look at me, starting to rise, until I put the flat of my hand on my stomach, twisting my face in distress.

He nodded, frowning in commiseration, as I turned away, edging past Mr. and Mrs. Abbot and starting down the stairs toward the exit.

(

It was almost completely dark in the big top, so I was a bit surprised, and relieved, that it was still light outside as I slipped through the entrance.

Not full light, but light enough. At least, that was what I hoped as I stopped and took a look around. There were a few people in the distance, circus workers moving about in the sudden emptiness of the grounds, but none nearby. Nobody to notice what I was doing, or to ask any questions as I looked at the ground, crouching slightly.

I had to find the coin. And this was my only chance. If I had dropped it inside the tent, in the crush, in the dark, there was no chance.

But if I dropped it outside . . .

I bent lower to the ground, narrowed my focus.

The grass was a trampled mess of cigarette butts and crushed wrappers, pink and blue stained cones from cotton candy, fragments of paper and, here and there, chicken bones and broken plastic utensils. Every time something caught the light just right I would lurch forward, hand extended, but it was never anything: a penny, half-buried in the crunched brown grass, a drying gob of spit . . .

"Are you looking for something?"

I sprang to my feet at the sound of the voice, my face flushing.

Zeffirelli was perched a short distance away on what looked like the stool that had been beside the gate to the sideshow.

My breath caught in my throat when I saw what he was doing with his hands.

The coin appeared in his right, disappeared in his left.

The coin, glistening in the slanted evening light.

"Do you always take such poor care with gifts you're given?" he asked, rising to his feet and stepping toward me.

I took an instinctive step back. "No," I said quietly, the shame burning through me. "I'm sorry, Mr. Zeffirelli. I didn't mean to—"

His smile broke through his goatee, his eyes filling with light. This was the Zeffirelli I recognized. This was the Zeffirelli I had met in the dugout.

"Please," he said, as if waving away my sadness. "You've done nothing wrong."

The coin flashed between his hands.

"Sometimes things are lost."

The coin vanished in his left hand, and I felt a pang of sadness, as if a light had gone out.

"There's no one to blame, no apologies to be made."

He shrugged. I waited for the coin to reappear.

"They just go. People. Places. Things. Everything disappears."

He kissed the fingertips of his right hand and gestured into the air, like setting something free.

There was no sign of the coin.

I looked at Zeffirelli's left hand, where the coin had last been. I looked to his right, as he lowered it to his side.

Nothing.

When I looked up, his eyes met mine.

"But sometimes," he said slowly, thoughtfully, "when all seems lost, we find something else. Something unexpected. Something beyond our imaginings." His voice was inviting.

Forgiving.

I felt the warmth of it wash through me.

"Would you care to go for a walk?" he asked, inclining his head slightly, as if anxious for my answer.

The question took me by surprise, and I glanced at the entrance to the tent. It didn't occur to me to say no; of course I would go with him.

But—

"Don't you have to be—" I didn't even finish the question—he was the ringmaster. Didn't he need to be inside the big top?

He smiled. "I have a little time," he said. "Come. There's something I want to show you."

Zeffirelli talked as we walked, pointing things out as we wended our way through the maze of trucks and trailers. "That's Bert's place," he said, pointing at the trailer with the painting of the bearded lady. "She goes by Roberta, but her friends all call her Bert. And that's . . ."

He was like a tour guide, and I was paying such close attention to what he was saying, what he was pointing out, that I quickly lost any sense of where I was, how I might find my way back out of the maze.

We walked for what seemed like hours, turning and turning, winding our way through the backstage world of the circus. Time seemed to lose all meaning. I thought of asking him, once or twice, if he should be getting back to the ring, but as quickly as the thought came to mind I dismissed it. It was his circus. He knew what he was doing.

And it wouldn't be long now. . . .

It was almost dark by the time we reached our destination, a rusty trailer in the center of the lot, parked next to the rusty red truck I had seen that morning on the road.

Had it really only been that morning? It seemed so much longer ago. Weeks. Months. Not mere hours.

He had to tug on the door before it opened with a dull pop. "Be it ever so humble," he said, stepping up and inside, flicking on a light. "Come in," he beckoned.

I stopped at the threshold when the reality of the situation exploded inside my brain. I didn't know him, at all. And he wanted me to come into his trailer? I didn't even need to think of my mother, holding a crumpled newspaper in her hand, waving it, tears in her eyes, as she warned me about strangers, about what someone had done to the little boys they had taken, to know that this was a bad idea.

"Um," I started, trying to figure out a way out of this. "Shouldn't you—" I gestured in what I thought was the direction of the big top. "Don't you need to be back?"

He smiled, wide and soft, as if he really did understand.

"You're a bright boy," he said. "Probably brighter than you're given credit for, a lot of the time."

It seemed like a question in his voice; I had no idea how to respond.

"I'll tell you what," he said, straightening to his full height. Something about the motion caused me to move back, and he stepped down from the doorway, back onto the grass, almost brushing my shoulder as he moved past me. "There's something you should see, inside. But I'll stay out here." He lowered his head, looked at me as if expecting an answer. "How does that sound?"

I was already leaning toward the doorway, craning my neck to see more of the inside. It was like the decision had already been made for me.

I took a step forward to the edge of the doorway. I looked at Zeffirelli Nodded. "Okay."

The next step took me up, and in.

I glanced back at Zeffirelli. He hadn't moved.

It was hot inside. Not quite what you would expect, being inside a tin can that had been roasting in the sun all day, but uncomfortable. The dimness helped, but I still broke into a sweat.

Although it was small, the trailer seemed roomy on the inside, clean and almost spacious. There was no clutter: a neat bookshelf with all the spines lined up, an open closet, the clothes hung with care, dark shirts and long jackets like the one he was wearing now. A tiny kitchen, tidy, no dishes or pots on the counter, circus posters on the wall above the tiny sink. It didn't look scary.

I glanced back toward him, then took a step deeper towards the back of the trailer.

There was a small table and a padded bench next to the kitchen area, a paperback book tented open next to a candle in the centre of the table. There were two doors toward the back of the trailer, both of them closed. I had been in a couple of trailers before; I knew that one of the doors led to a tiny bathroom, the other to a sleeping area, a bedroom that would probably be all mattress on a platform over a storage area. All the dressing and getting ready for the day would happen out here.

I let my gaze fall across Zeffirelli as I turned, trying not to look like I was checking on him. When he started to smile, I swung my gaze away, toward the front of the trailer, and froze, my breath sticking in my throat.

A boy my age was standing at the far end of the room.

I jumped back, made a small sound.

The boy jumped back, his lips moving.

"Are you all right?" Zeffirelli stepped toward the door. Stopped.

"I'm okay." I waved my hand toward him, as if to keep him out of his own trailer.

The boy moved his hand dismissively.

"It's a mirror," Zeffirelli said.

"I know."

But it wasn't, quite.

At least, not like any mirror I had ever seen. The mirror was huge, spanning the entire front wall of the trailer. There was no frame, nothing to clearly mark the dimensions of the glass. Standing in the living area, it was impossible to see both edges of the mirror at the same time; you had to turn your head slightly to orient yourself.

I took a step forward; the boy stepped forward toward me. I lifted my left hand. The boy lifted his right. I clenched my raised fist. The boy clenched his.

The boy was clearly me, but also not, in the way a reflection is always fleetingly confusing, never quite matching up to the image we carry in our heads. The boy in the mirror seemed taller somehow than I imagined myself, his face thinner, his eyes brighter.

But that was just the way mirrors worked.

Except . . .

My reflection was standing in a different room.

I took a full turn, looking around the trailer.

Nothing made sense.

The reflected room looked about the same size, the close corners and angles suggesting that it might also be a trailer, but everything else was completely different. There was no trace of the kitchen counter, or the fixed benches along the walls with their squared cushions.

Instead of the doorways to the bedroom and bathroom, the room ended in a beaded curtain, containing the space, creating a feeling of warmth, of safety, a feeling that the orange light of the flickering candles only added to. There was a rug on the floor, an ornate Persian pattern like something out of the *Arabian Nights*, scattered with large cushions, around a low table on which a lantern burned. The walls were hung with—

Behind my reflection, the beaded curtain parted and Zeferelli stepped into the room.

I whirled around, raising my hands defensively.

The trailer was empty. The light above the sink burned with a steady, sharp light.

"Mr. Zeffirelli?" I called out, tying to force my voice not to shake.

"It's all right," he said, from outside the trailer. "I've kept my word."

I stared at the doorway for a long moment, making sure he wasn't lying, then turned back to the mirror, my reflection.

He—I had already started to think of him as a he, something not me—hadn't turned when I had. He remained standing stock still, staring at me. Zeffirelli had stepped close behind him, his hand on my reflection's shoulder.

For a moment, I could almost feel the hand on myself, but I blinked heavily, forced the feeling away.

"What the hell?"

He raised his eyes to look at me, as if he had heard. I thought it had to be a trick, some sort of stage magic that Zeffirelli kept in his trailer to freak people out. Something to do with screens and mirrors and corners. Some sort of trick.

"Mr. Zeffirelli," I called out as I stepped toward the mirror. There had to be some trick. If I could just figure it out—

As my fingers brushed the cool surface of the mirror, the world lurched under my feet, a tremor so sudden and severe it buckled my knees. I clamped my eyes shut, squeezed down hard, breathing slow through my nose to right myself, to try to keep from throwing up.

When I was finally able to open my eyes, I almost doubled over.

At first, for a fleeting moment, I thought that everything was all right, that things were back to normal.

But I was wrong.

The air was different, smelling of citrus and spices, the orange light wavering, as if from candles. The mirror now reflected the doors to the bedroom and the bathroom, the kitchen nook, the book on the table.

And I could feel the weight of Zeffirelli's hand on my shoulder. For real.

I whirled around, stepped back, the carpet so thick under my feet that I almost fell.

Zeffirelli raised his hands, palms open and facing me. "It's all right," he said. "That's a perfectly normal response."

I shifted my eyes between him and the room on the other side of the mirror. My reflection's hand was extended, his fingers touching the surface of the mirror, his brow knit tight with confusion, fear in his eyes as they almost met mine.

"I understand you're confused," Zeffirelli said.

For some reason, the smooth, soothing calm of his voice only served to put me more on edge. I took another step back, compensating for the softness of the carpet underfoot by flexing my knees.

"What's going on? What is this place?"

"It's the other side of the mirror," Zeffirelli said. Not the Zeffirelli standing behind me, but the Zeffirelli who stood in the doorway of the trailer behind my reflection. Me. The other me. I couldn't tell if he was answering my question, or anticipating what the other version of me was about to ask.

I looked at myself, waited for him to speak.

He didn't. He just half-closed his eyes and nodded, not because the explanation made sense, or that he understood, but because he was powerless, that mute acceptance was the only response.

Something about his expression cut through me, lit something inside me that felt like a fuse.

"That's not an answer," I said, looking at the Zeffirelli in the glass but directing the comment at the Zeffirelli a few steps away from me. "How did I get here?"

"You've always been here," Zeffirelli said, the Zeffirelli that was closest to me.

This Zeffirelli was tall, his moustache and goatee thick, his jacket smooth and heavy, no errant threads, no tattered edges. The flower in his pocket was lush, its scent rich and heavy.

"That's not an answer either," I said, half-turning toward him.

"Isn't it?" the Zeffirelli on the other side of the glass said. He stepped toward the mirror as he—the other me—turned toward him, both stopping to stand in almost the same positions as we did on our side of the mirror.

"Jesus," I muttered.

My reflection swallowed.

I reached up, touched the tip of my nose like I was scratching it. The other me touched his nose, then looked at me, a scowl on his face.

I knew what he was thinking: he was mentally ordering me to stop, saying that he was in control of his actions, that he would scratch his nose when he felt like it, not when—

"But mirrors are the same on both sides," I said.

"Usually," Zeffirelli said, on the other side of the glass.

I watched myself sigh with exasperation.

"No," the other me said, chopping decisively at the air with the edge of his right hand. "Always. That's what makes them mirrors."

"That's what makes *some* mirrors," Zeffirelli said from my side of the glass.

"What?" my reflection and I said, at the same time.

Both Zeffirellis smiled.

"Have you ever caught a glimpse of yourself in a window at night?" the Zeffirelli on the other side of the glass asked.

"Or looked at your reflection in a still pond, like old Narcissus?" asked the one on mine.

My other self nodded as I said a careful "Yes."

And for a moment, I was at the edge of the pond in Miller's woods. It was a spring day, the sun high overhead, the sky a deep blue behind me, leaves thick and green, a light breeze tossing my hair as I leaned over the water, a space in my front teeth as I grinned.

For a moment, I caught sight of myself in the window behind the kitchen table. Mom and dad were talking, and I had turned in my chair, trying not to hear, meeting my eyes in the glass.

"Is what you see reflected always what's there?" the other Zeffirelli asked.

"Of course," both versions of me said, at the same moment.

"Really?" both Zeffirellis asked. "Look closer."

But I didn't need him to tell me. Didn't need the reminder. The breeze playing across the surface of the pond distorted my image, swirled sky and leaves together, and through my own face, through the blue above and behind me, I could see the shape of leaves under the surface, the shadow of the bottom of the pond somewhere distant, the shadows of unseen depth lurking just beyond my face yet somehow also within it, beyond the leaves and sky.

Beyond my face, the darkness outside the window was almost complete. The kitchen was bright, reflected in the glass, but even mom and dad seemed far away, indistinct, like the whole world was being pulled, helpless, into the darkness beyond the glass, the darkness just behind my face, my eyes.

We both nodded slowly.

"Okay," my reflection said, as if bracing himself for whatever Zeffirelli was going to say next.

The Zeffirelli on my side shook his head. "No," he said. "What did you see?"

The other me looked confused.

"In the glass," the other Zeffirelli said.

"In the pond," the Zeffirelli on my side of the glass said.

When we answered, I wasn't sure which of us said what.

"The bottom of the pond—"

"The dark outside—"

"And the shadows and plants—"

"It seemed to be trying to come in—"

Both Zeffirellis nodded thoughtfully.

"You were there too, in the glass, in the pond," they said.

We hesitated, then nodded. Of course.

"But how do you know," the Zeffirelli on my side of the glass said.

"Which of you is real,"

"And which is the reflection?"

It took me a moment to realize that I was standing in the plain trailer again, looking at the ornate, rich world through the mirror on the wall.

A sudden feeling of loss gusted through me like wind through a thin coat, a cold so severe I almost fell to my knees.

"Is the world around you the real one,"

"Or is it the world you see through the glass?"

"Is there a real world at all?"

I was in the candle-lit room again, the light warm and flickering, the carpet thick.

"Or is it all what you choose to see?"

"Is the darkness around you?"

"Or is it in the glass?"

"All right," I said, lifting my head. "Stop. I get it."

The Zeffirelli on my side of the glass smiled. "What do you get?"

I swallowed, looked at my reflection for support.

"There are two of me," I said slowly, looking at my own features, bracing myself for another correction.

Instead, he said, "Yes." Low and slow. "Are they the same?"

I said "Yes," though it felt like a guess, like it had to be wrong, like it was too easy somehow.

But he didn't correct me. "And what about the rest of what you see? The rooms, the people. Are they the same?"

I shook my head. "No." Almost confident that I was right this time.

"Of course," he said. I took a strange pleasure in having pleased him.

"Now," he said, slowly. "Which one is real?"

I froze. I knew what the answer had to be.

I thought of Bob waiting for me in the bleachers, the ride home on his bike, school starting in just over a week. Bob leaving. Mom and dad.

The answer was obvious.

But . . .

I could smell the oranges and spices, feel the heat of the candles, the softness of the rugs underfoot. . . .

I shook my head.

"Both?" I said carefully, knowing that I couldn't possibly be right.

Zeffirelli smiled. "Exactly," he said.

"But I don't—" I lifted my hand, reached toward the glass, touched my own fingers reaching toward me. "Are you saying I can just—" I fought for the right word. "—cross? I can go back and forth?"

Zeffirelli blinked heavily, and shook his head. My heart fell into the pit of my stomach.

"I'm sorry," he said, looking at me gravely. "Narcissus drowned, trying to reach his reflection. And putting yourself through a window . . ." He trailed off, leaving a picture in my mind of blood and shattered glass.

"But I just did." I gestured at the mirror.

"Here," said the Zeffirelli on my side. "And now."

"Only here," the other Zeffirelli echoed. "And only now."

"So when you leave—" I gestured at the candle-lit room behind me. "This will all be gone."

"That depends on what you choose."

His words seemed to hang in the air, to echo inside my head.

The Zeffirelli on the other side of the glass nodded. "One world seems more real to you now because it's the only world you've ever know. The other—" he gestured at the glass between us. "—is a mystery. But—" His eyes shone. "A world of wonder awaits, I can assure you."

Awaits?

"What are you saying?" The words seemed to pile up in the back of my throat. "Are you saying I can . . . Are you asking me to stay?"

"If you like."

I bit my lip, looked at myself in the glass. I could stay on the candle side. Here. With Zeffirelli. With the lions. With the circus.

I imagined someone saying, *He did it, he really did it. He ran away and joined the circus*, and in the mirror a smile broke over my face. But then the line registered with me, and I watched my face fall.

I couldn't do it. There wasn't any choice. Not really.

"What's wrong?" Zeffirelli asked.

"My mom and dad," I said. "My cousin Bob. Everyone in town. I can't just—" I struggled to find the right word. "Leave. Disappear."

For a moment, Zeffirelli seemed puzzled. Then he smiled. "Ah," he said. "I understand your difficulty." He pulled lightly on his beard. "Coming with us won't mean leaving. Not really."

My reflection frowned, his forehead creasing in puzzlement.

"When the circus goes in the morning, this trailer, this mirror, will lead the caravan. The mirror, and everything it contains, will be gone. But there will always be a you, here, in this little town. He will live his life as it was going to be lived, on that side of the glass. On this side . . ." He shrugged slightly. "Who knows what wonders await a boy your age?" He put his hand on my shoulder. "You have to decide which side of the glass you will live within. Which side will be real to you, and which will become a dream, a path not taken."

I nodded slowly.

The Zeffirelli on the other side of the glass lifted his head. "I must tell you, though: time grows short. Our stay in your little town is almost at an end."

Fear twisted the features of my reflection, uncertainty in his eyes. I couldn't look away. "What if I make the wrong choice? What if I change my mind? I'm only eleven years old!"

Zeffirelli shook his head slowly. "Ten, eleven, twenty, forty," he said. "Everyone decides." He reached into the air and plucked a coin out of the nothing. "But not everyone realizes it, at the time." He shrugged, and snapped his fingers, and the coin disappeared.

My reflection sagged.

"But I'm only eleven," I repeated. "How should I know what to do?"

{

When I woke up the next morning, I didn't know where I was.

Everything seemed strange, uncomfortable. It took me a long moment to understand why: I was still dressed, still wearing the same clothes I had worn to the circus.

The circus . . .

The thought of the night before brought a slight pounding to my head, a grating throb in my temples, and I shut my eyes again, tried to count my breaths.

When the feeling began to recede, I opened my eyes again. I was in my room. I was in my bed. But I couldn't remember how I got there.

It was only when I tried to sit up that I realized: I wasn't *in* my bed, I was *on* it, on top of the blankets and comforter.

How did I get there?

And why was it so bright? The sky outside the window above my desk was heavy with thick, grey-black clouds, but the room was bright. It was almost like—

"Oh no."

My clock read 11:17.

I stood bolt upright and crossed the room in three steps, leaning over my desk to look out the window. The driveway was empty. The world looked cool, and steely, like the edge of rain, the leaves on the nut trees that ran along the edge of the east fields rippling with a breeze I couldn't hear or feel.

The house was still, an emptiness that I had come to recognize.

I straightened up, and it all came back to me in a rush. I remembered the beginning of the circus, the lions coming into the big top. I remembered standing up, motioning to Bob that I had to leave, that I had to go to the bathroom. I remembered how cool the tile wall of the stall had felt against the side of my head as I perched on the toilet, sweat soaking my face. My shirt. I remembered the sound of the restroom door opening, and Bob's voice, quiet, concerned, calling my name, asking if I was all right. And I wasn't.

As I looked around the room, the gaps in my memory started to fill in. I spotted the bucket on the floor by the head of the bed. Bob had borrowed John Horvath's car, had laid me in the back seat. He had carried me into the house, and up the stairs. He had sat on the edge of the bed, rubbing my back, as I fell asleep.

The thought of it made me smile. At the same time, it made me sad. I had missed most of the circus. I exhaled through my nose, and took a deep breath. Thought about Bob. Tried to be cool. It was all right. The circus would come back, maybe next summer. There would be another chance.

I was still weak and a little woozy from being sick, and my whole body felt strangely tender, but staying in bed really wasn't an option. I needed to put on my work clothes and get out there.

My hands shook slightly, and it took me a moment to unbuckle my belt. As I pulled off my pants, something fell out of my pocket, striking the floor with a hollow clatter and slipping under my desk.

I reached into the shadows and pulled out a plastic disk about the size and weight of a bingo chip. The gold finish was chipped and pitted, but I could still make out the circular logo of the circus.

I smiled as I stood up. A token or something. Maybe from one of the games. I wondered, for a moment, where I had got it, then I dropped it on my desk with a small clatter. I'd put it away somewhere when I got in from my chores. The circus would be back, and I would be able to use it then, whatever it was.

But in the meantime . . .

I could almost hear my father's voice cutting in.

. . . daylight was burning, and there was a farm to run. Chores to be done.

We worked through most of the night.

After the crowds dispersed, after the temporary gates had been locked, the hands brought out the lights and we started to tear down the show. We worked from the outside in: the trailers with the games were the first to go, the machinery stowed, the doors closed and bolted, the trailers driven off to form the beginnings of a line down the side of the straight country road.

The sideshow and the food tents were next. I wanted to help out with the sideshow, just for a glimpse of what was behind the golden rope, but Zeffirelli held me back, shaking his head. "There'll be time enough for that," he said, before sending me off to work on the cotton candy machine.

The big top was last. For that I just stood back and watched, keeping a safe distance as the hands brought the tent down with a whoosh of canvas-smelling air and an odd popping noise. Watching it sag, watching them roll it up, was as exhilarating as it had been to see it towering above the agricultural grounds the day before.

Had it only been a day? It felt like so much longer.

After that, we slept for a few hours. Zeffirelli frowned apologetically as he laid out a blanket on the bench in the trailer's kitchen. "We'll find you a spot in one of the trailers tonight," he said. "But for now, you can crash here, all right?"

I just nodded. I hadn't said much since the night before, when I watched my other self walk away the night before, his shoulders hunched, his head low. It didn't seem like there was a whole lot to say.

I glanced at the mirror once before I fell asleep, just to check. The glass only reflected the trailer around me. Zeffirelli's trailer. Mine, for the night.

A few hours later, barely awake, I stumbled into the passenger seat of Zeffirelli's truck, closed the door behind me. We pulled out first, before I even had my seatbelt fastened, and moved at a crawl up the road, letting the other trucks and trailers fall in behind us. Zeffirelli kept checking his rearview mirror, and only when he was sure everyone was in place did he put his foot on the gas.

The engine roared loudly.

I watch the outskirts of the little town spool by, waiting. Everything looked different from inside the truck. Smaller, somehow. Grey, like it might start to rain at any moment.

And then we were passing open fields, rows of corn, hay as high as a boy's thighs, all blowing in a slight breeze.

To my right, there was a small cream house, set back from the road by a vegetable garden, a motorcycle in the driveway. And just past that, more fields, hay again, but pasture this time, a dozen cows ambling toward the barn, herded by a young boy with messy brown hair and dirty jeans, shooing them along with a switch.

The boy looked up at the caravan as we passed, and I raised my hand to him through the glass, but I don't think he saw.

And then we were past, and he was gone.

SOME NOTES ON STORIES, SHORT AND OTHERWISE

The stories in this collection span about three decades, which, truth be told, is something of an alarming thought. The oldest were written about twenty-five years ago (an odd thing, that, considering, in my head, I've just turned twenty-five myself), while the most recent was finished about a month ago.

Because I consider myself primarily a novelist, I was surprised to find, when I started pulling this book together, that I actually had quite a stack of stories to decide between for inclusion. This, however, isn't an exhaustive collection, and that's my fault. And all because of a poem.

The title for the book, and its form (however rough), comes from the old English counting rhyme. People have been counting crows (or magpies) for hundreds of years now, and there are a number of variations, but all of the rhymes follow a general structure. The version that has guided me is:

One for sorrow
Two for mirth
Three for a wedding
Four for a birth
Five for silver
Six for gold
Seven for a secret
Never to be told

The idea of secrets, never to be told, stuck with me. Crows. Secrets. Stories.

Seven Crow Stories.

With that in mind, and as a guiding principle, I knew what the collection would look like: seven stories.

As a result, there are a number of stories that aren't here. And it's not just a matter of space. I sought, through the selection process, to avoid undue repetition of themes (hence no "Fiddler's Green," no "The Ones He Used to Know"), and there are stories that just didn't fit, for one reason or another ("Coming To Land"). And there are stories that started out as stories and ended up as . . . something else.

I am not, by nature, a short-story writer. I approach a story in exactly the same way I approach a novel, which is a path fraught with peril. "Peril" in this case referring to the fact that, fairly often, pieces which I thought would be short stories turn into novels, as happened with *The Fallow Heart*, which started out as a novella a couple of decades ago and is currently a sprawling manuscript, more than novel length, spread out etherized on my revision table. Similarly, a couple of years ago I started writing a novella which has, somehow, turned into a trilogy, in progress. So it goes.

Most of the time, I can tell, even in its germinal state, whether an idea is going to turn into a story or a novel. It's pretty straightforward: stories don't stay. Like most novelists (I think), I can carry a notion for a novel with me for weeks, years if need be, niggling at the back of my head, accruing weight, until it becomes an irresistible force.

Ideas for stories aren't like that. Generally, if I have an idea for a story, I need to leap on it right away, or it disappears. I need to write it within about seventy-two hours, or it dissipates, back into the vapours. Jotting down the concept isn't enough; if I don't get to it right away, it's gone, and any notes I might have made are inert, lacking the primal force that drives the pen. I don't know why it works like that, but it does. And I'm glad. That's how I knew there was more to "Winter's Tale" than the long short story I wrote: it kept haunting me, pulling at me, until I gave it another look. And lo, *Black Feathers* was born.

At any rate, I went through the stack of stories, and came up with a rough selection for this book. And then I had to fight against every natural writerly instinct I have, and step back.

With a time span of twenty five years, there's a lot of stylistic variation here, and I wanted to smooth it out. I had to resist that urge.

Because stories don't stay, and because each story is written in a gush, every story is, to me, something of a peculiar marker, a glimpse of where I was as I was writing, who I was at that particular moment. I wouldn't write, say, "Blessing" the same way today, nor should I. The story exists the way it is because of the way I was at the time I was inspired, at the time I was writing.

The revision process was, therefore, at times, counter-intuitive, more akin to archeology than to my usual process. My goal wasn't to make these stories conform to where I am now, as a writer, but to gingerly dust them off, clean them up, and present them into the light. There were a couple of exceptions. "Coming to Land" isn't here because there are parts of it that made me wince, and wonder about the kid who wrote it (and also because there's more to that story. That one has stuck with me, which leads me to believe . . . well, you know.) And "The Last Circus"? Well, we'll come to that.

So. Seven secrets. Seven stories.

Almost.

"Grateful" isn't formally part of *Seven Crow Stories*, but I knew, from the start, that it had to be here, an introduction of sorts. For the longest time, I referred to "Grateful" as "The Storyteller's Story," which I think says it all (but that's not going to stop me from writing a bit more).

"Grateful" is one of the oldest stories in this book, written in the early 1990s, almost immediately after I decided I wouldn't go to grad school, choosing to focus on my writing instead. In a way, it's the most autobiographical story in the book, despite not being autobiographical in the slightest. I don't drive, I've never met a ghost (much to my chagrin), I never trained to be a teacher. . . . And yet . . . Like Murray in the story, "Grateful" was where I burned my boats.

The story comes from a folktale motif referred to as "the grateful dead," in which a traveler assists a stranger, who turns out to be the spirit of one recently departed, and receives a boon for their assistance. That motif, obviously, was the inspiration for the band's name; the story was actually inspired by the title and the opening line of the Dead's "I Will Take You Home"—"Little girl lost, in a forest of dreams."

Two other things: if you think Murray seems familiar, it may be because you've met him, in the pages of *Black Feathers*. And you'll see him again, I promise.

And finally: "Grateful" was first published in a textbook anthology for high school students, which, given its subject matter, is perfect, and, given my fraught relationship with my own high school experience, is more than a little delightful.

"Tom Chesnutt's Midnight Blues" was written, I believe, in 2008, after I had made the acquaintance of one Marla Good, who is a font of often deeply disturbing story inspirations and elements. I try to get together with Marla when I'm in Toronto, and I always bring a notebook with me.

Beyond the basics, I often don't know where the elements of a story come from, but with Tom C., I have a few signposts. His experiences in Spokane, Washington are drawn from a day I spent there on the US tour for *Before I Wake*, while the bar he plays in Victoria is the late, lamented Harpo's.

And if you think Collette seems familiar, it's likely because she too appears in the pages of *Black Feathers* (the party, where Cassie talks to Murray, is held in Collette's apartment, upstairs from Ali's basement suite). You will find, as we go on, that these sorts of connections are the rule, rather than the exception, and definitely by design.

In keeping with the music/music industry setting and themes, I have always viewed "Crossroads Blues" as the B-side to "Tom Chesnutt" (to the point that I've actually thought of printing them as a chapbook, front to back, so you have to flip the "record" over to read the other story).

The inspiration here, I think, is obvious: "Crossroads Blues" is one of the most famous of the tracks bluesman Robert Johnson recorded after (allegedly) selling his soul to the devil, a legend which Charlie Webber is perhaps too familiar with. And the devil, well, he clearly has a sense of humour. Or irony, at least.

I'm not normally a night writer—I prefer the pre-dawn for fiction—but in mid-2011 I was at my desk at about ten at night, finishing the typing of the first draft of "The Crying in the Walls," when the line "I sold my soul to the devil in the parking lot of a 7-Eleven" popped unbidden into my head. I finished the typing and wrote "Crossroads Blues" in one sitting, knowing nothing more about the story, its structure, its characters, than that single line, and that voice. . . . Oh, that voice.

"Blessing" is one of the oldest stories in this collection, written around the same time as "Grateful." I recall, at the time, experimenting with what I thought of as a "storyteller's voice," trying to create a "once upon a time" story without the "once upon a time." It's significant, I think, that out of that experiment came the first story set in Henderson; it was, from the very beginning, a place out of fable, out of fairy tale.

In this story we meet, for the first time, John and Claire Joseph, and other residents of the town, people we'll come to know, and love, and mourn, in stories to come. You've been warned.

"The Crying in the Walls" is my one and only (so far) Toronto story. In part, it's the architecture: we don't have semi-detached houses out here in the wild west (we have duplexes, which aren't the same), and I needed to have that adjoining wall. Mostly, though, it's due to spending afternoons with James Grainger, walking around his old neighbourhood, looking at buildings and talking about horror.

"Three Days Gone" occupies a strange space in my head. It's a finished short story; it does exactly what I want it to do, it moves, it breathes . . . It might also be the first chapter of a trilogy of novels. I like to think it's done, but only time will tell. . . .

I'm not sure if this was written before or after *The World More Full of Weeping* (I suspect before), but there are certainly elements in common: lost children, other worlds, the lives of those left behind. These are some of the things I keep coming back to, and I'm not sure why. I'm not sure I want to find out.

I wrote a bit about "The Small Rain Down" when it was published in the limited edition of *The World More Full of Weeping*, so I may just quote myself: "In late October 2006 I sat down with the deliberate intention of writing an 'October' story, something suffused with death, and loss, and dreams; the story equivalent of the smell of leaves burning in the distance and the slow, autumnal dwindling of days. To that end, I pulled out a Moleskine notebook (with that earthy cream paper) and a Lamy Al-Star loaded with Noodler's Walnut ink (a deep, earthy brown) and set to work. The story was written in virtually a single sitting, over the course of a rainy weekend, with the house to myself, a leaking roof, and Nick Drake's *Way to Blue* on repeat on the CD player. It might just be me, but I think you can hear the rain, and the slow, sad music, in the spaces between the words."

Which almost says it all, save this: looking at it now, as part of this selection of my work, "The Small Rain Down" seems, in part, to be an answer to a question that "Grateful" almost asks, but doesn't quite. Or that might just be me.

Tracking down the dates for some of these stories has been a bit tricky; not so with "The Last Circus"; I finished writing this story in early August, 2016, after several months of stop-and-start writing. Though that's not the whole truth. . . .

This version of "The Last Circus" is actually a second version of the same inspiration, my memories of the day the circus came to town, when I was about twelve years old. In a way, this is an autobiographical story, but then, it would be, whether you lived it or not. There's a mirror for us all.

All writers carry their influences with them, sometimes in their hearts, sometimes on their sleeves. I wrote this, very consciously, with Ray Bradbury in mind, the way he could make a circus wonderful and terrifying at the same time.

I knew, though, without even looking at the earlier version of the story, that I hadn't quite said what I wanted to say with the story, so I decided to revisit the material. As near as I can figure, the first version of the story was written in the mid '90s, so this version is twenty years down the road. The same story, but utterly different.

The same, I suppose, can be said about me, twenty years on: the same story, but utterly different. I don't know when I crossed over into the mirror world, or how many times, but that's the secret, I suppose. Never to be told.

PUBLICATION HISTORY

"The Small Rain Down"—limited edition hardcover of *The World More Full of Weeping*, ChiZine Publications, 2009

"Grateful"—*Reality Imagined: Stories of Identity and Change*, McGraw-Hill Ryerson, 2011

"Tom Chesnutt's Midnight Blues"—*Chilling Tales: Evil Did I Dwell; Lewd Did I Live*, EDGE Science Fiction and Fantasy, 2011

"Crossroads Blues"—*Chilling Tales: In Words, Alas, Drown I*, EDGE Science Fiction and Fantasy, 2013

"The Last Circus"—Found Press, 2016

"Blessing," "The Crying in the Walls," and "Three Days Gone" are original to this collection.

ACKNOWLEDGEMENTS

I am grateful to the venues in which some of these stories first appeared, and thankful for the skills and attention of their editors, including Jared Bland, Michael Kelly, Bryan Jay Ibeas, and, of course, Brett Savory and Sandra Kasturi at ChiZine, for that and for this.

Thanks to Samantha Beiko, who oversaw this book with diligence and care. And, it should be said, infinite patience. I swear, it's almost finished.

I am grateful to everyone at the McDermid Agency, in a world of ways, but special thanks to Chris Bucci and, as always, Anne McDermid.

With stories spanning more than twenty years, it's inevitable I'll miss someone, but I am grateful to Marla Good, Clare Hitchens, James Grainger, Colin Holt, the members of the now-gone Yahoo group, and so many others, for early reads, inspiration, pep talks, drunken commiserating, walking tours and the like.

Special thanks to Cori Dusmann, of course.

Love and gratitude to August, who keeps me simultaneously grounded and on my toes, as only a seventeen-year-old can.

And finally, my deepest thanks to Athena McKenzie. No dress rehearsal, only second acts.

ABOUT THE AUTHOR

ROBERT J. WIERSEMA is a writer of fiction and non-fiction, and a reviewer who contributes regularly to several national newspapers. He is the best-selling author of three novels: *Before I Wake*, *Bedtime Story*, and *Black Feathers*, as well as the mix-tape memoir *Walk Like a Man: Coming of Age with the Music of Bruce Springsteen*. He teaches creative writing at Vancouver Island University, and lives in Victoria, British Columbia.

EMB
RACE
THE
ODD